Specific Skills

Place Value

by
April Duff, M.Ed.
and
Leland Graham, Ph.D.

illustrated by
Janet Armbrust

Level 2

900
800
700
600
500
400
300
200
100

Publisher
Key Education Publishing Company, LLC
Minneapolis, Minnesota

www.keyeducationpublishing.com

CONGRATULATIONS ON YOUR PURCHASE OF A KEY EDUCATION PRODUCT!

The editors at Key Education are former teachers who bring experience, enthusiasm, and quality to each and every product. Thousands of teachers have looked to the staff at Key Education for new and innovative resources to make their work more enjoyable and rewarding. We are committed to developing educational materials that will assist teachers in building a strong and developmentally appropriate curriculum for young children.

PLAN FOR GREAT TEACHING EXPERIENCES WHEN YOU USE EDUCATIONAL MATERIALS FROM KEY EDUCATION PUBLISHING COMPANY, LLC!

About the Authors

Dr. Leland Graham is a former college professor, principal, and teacher, who was twice voted "Outstanding Teacher of the Year." The author of 55 educational books, Dr. Graham is a popular speaker and workshop presenter throughout Georgia and the USA, as well as a presenter for NSSEA (National School Supply & Equipment Association). Thousands of teachers have benefited from his workshops on reading, math, and improving achievement scores.

April Duff is a literacy support teacher for Even Start in Burke County, Georgia. She has a M.Ed. in reading, language and literacy education from Georgia State University and a B.S. in early childhood education from Georgia College and State University. She has also taught fourth grade and kindergarten, and has served as an IEP Reading and Math Specialist for grades 1–5. Ms. Duff lives in Georgia, and enjoys reading and traveling.

Acknowledgments

The authors would like to acknowledge the assistance of the following educators: Jean Anderson and Barry Doran, Math Coordinators from DeKalb County School System, Decatur, Georgia, and David Park, proofreader.

Credits
Authors: April Duff, M.Ed. and Leland Graham, Ph.D.
Publisher: Sherrill B. Flora
Illustrator: Janet Armbrust
Editors: Debra Pressnall and George C. Flora
Cover Design: Annette Hollister-Papp
Page Design and Layout: Swan Johnson
Cover Photographs: © Brand X Pictures and © Photodisc

Key Education welcomes manuscripts and product ideas from teachers. For a copy of our submission guidelines, please send a self-addressed, stamped envelope to:

Key Education Publishing Company, LLC
Acquisitions Department
9601 Newton Avenue South
Minneapolis, Minnesota 55431

Copyright Notice
No part of this publication may be reproduced or transmitted by any means (electronic, mechanical, photocopy, recording) or stored in any information storage or retrieval system without the prior written permission of the publisher. Reproducible pages (student activity sheets and patterns) may be duplicated by the classroom teacher for use in the classroom but may not be reproduced for commercial sale. Reproduction for an entire school system is strictly prohibited. For information regarding permission, write to: **Permissions, Key Education Publishing Company, LLC, 9601 Newton Avenue South, Minneapolis, Minnesota 55431.**

Standard Book Number: 1-933052-51-1
Specific Skills: Place Value — Level 2
Copyright © 2007 by Key Education Publishing Company, LLC
Minneapolis, Minnesota 55431

Printed in the USA • All rights reserved

Table of Contents

Introduction 4

Support Materials

Pretest/Posttest... 5–6
Place Value for Parents 7
Using Manipulatives and Number Charts..... 8
Turtle Ten-Frame Grids 9
Hippo Hundred Board 10
Number Charts: 1–100, 101–200 11
Number Charts: 201–300, 301–400 12

Place Value 1-999

Matching Sets 13
Tens and Ones 14
Drivers, Find Your Cars! 15
Crow About These Numbers! 16
Is It Odd or Even? 17
Greater Than, Less Than, Equal To 18
Big Fish 19
Cool Counting by 10s.................................. 20
Winning Numbers 21
Taking a Hike! 22
Counting Hundreds and Tens..................... 23
Charting Hundreds, Tens, and Ones 24
Picture These Number Clues!..................... 25
You Make the Picture! 26
Sidewalk Block Math 27
Riddle My Numbers 28
What Comes Before or After?..................... 29
Picturing Between Numbers 30
One More Time . . . >, <, or =...................... 31
Ordering Numbers...................................... 32
Stretch Out Numbers.................................. 33
Snap Up Numbers! 34
Less and More... 35
Where Is the 4? 36
And the Number Is 37

Practical Applications

Base-Ten Model Patterns 38
Hands-On Addition...................................... 39
Adding with Place Value Chart 40
Adding with Regrouping 41
Hands-On Subtraction 42
Subtracting with Place Value Chart 43
Subtracting with Regrouping...................... 44

Partner Games to Play

Directions for Partner Games 45–46
Counting On Logs/Fly-In 400
Game Pieces...47
Counting On Logs Game Board.................. 48
Fly-In 400 Game Board 49
Unlock the Tens Game Pieces 50–52
Blast Off! Game Board 53
Blast Off! Game Cards 54
Ten Dollars and Ten Cents Game Board 55
Ten Dollars and Ten Cents Game Pieces.... 56

Other Resources

Money, Money! A Center Activity..................57
Numbers Rule! A Center Activity 58–59
Place Value Flash Cards 60–61
Web Sites... 62
Answer Key..63–64

Introduction

In *Specific Skills: Place Value* you will find a collection of reproducible math activities, pattern pages, and easy-to-play learning games to help students, especially struggling learners, develop an understanding of base-ten concepts and number quantities. Each book in this series also includes assessment opportunities in the form of a pretest/posttest, which has been formatted according to national standards. A special feature in this series is the "Place Value for Parents" letter. This reproducible handout incorporates math-related literature with fun at-home activities to further enhance the child's understanding of place value. The authors believe that the letter will also encourage parental involvement. Finally, provided in the back of each resource book is a list of Web sites that may be useful to teachers and parents. Some of the Web sites are information based, which may be helpful in designing lesson plans. Other Web sites offer place value games that children will enjoy playing while learning number concepts at the same time.

Specific Skills: Place Value — Level 2 is aligned with NCTM (National Council of Teachers of Mathematics) Standards. The practice pages and partner games can be used in a variety of ways, including whole group lessons, independent student work, or as enrichment activities at home. Based on various standards, the activities cover the following essential math skills:

- Naming and writing numerals 1–999
- Counting ones, tens, and hundreds
- Using expanded notation
- Ordering and comparing numbers
- Adding and subtracting two- and three-digit numbers with regrouping

Now that children have had many experiences in building number quantities up to 100, they are ready to discover how the base-ten number system works for larger numbers. In the Level 2 activities and games, children will be introduced to the concept of the hundred-grid (also known as a flat in a proportional base-ten set) and how 10 hundred-grids represent 1000. To help children internalize this concept, it is important that they have many opportunities to build numbers up to 400 first with actual objects before using paper-models to represent even larger numbers. As their level of understanding advances, students may enjoy playing the games "Counting On Logs" and "Fly-In 400." Being able to skip count by 100 from any number is one of the objectives of the game "Unlock the Tens." Another concept that children will be expected to master is showing the expanded form for numbers up to 999. This skill is the focus of the game "Blast-Off!" Finally, the game "Ten Dollars and Ten Cents" offers a different twist for helping children internalize the concepts of exchanging 10 tens for 100 and 10 hundreds for 1000. Learning about place value concepts can be fun, and more easily mastered, with activities and games!

Name _____   Date _____

Pretest/Posttest

Directions: Circle the correct answers.

1. What is the number?

hundreds	tens	ones
1	2	3

   A. 213   B. 123   C. 321

2. I am an **even** number between 25 and 30. What number am I?

   A. 26   B. 27   C. 29

3. Which number matches the written form?

   eight hundred seventy-five

   A. 8,705   B. 800,705   C. 875

4. What number is shown?

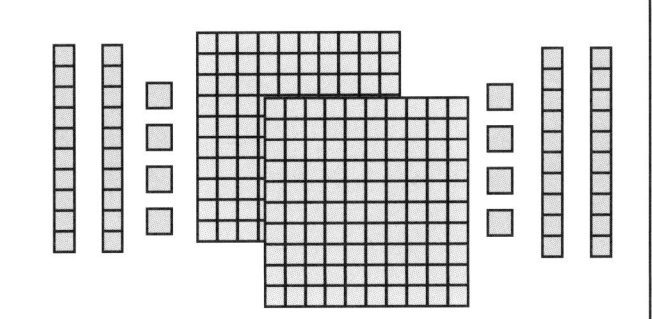

   A. 2,408   B. 1,424   C. 248

5. Identify the standard form of the number given.

   300 + 40 + 3

   A. 343   B. 30,043   C. 3,043

6. Which number comes between these two numbers?

   998, ____, 1,000

   A. 997   B. 999   C. 996

Name _____   Date _____

Pretest/Posttest

Directions: Circle the correct answers.

---

7. The following numbers are in order from least to greatest. What is the missing number?

   267, 329, ___, 403

   A. 356   B. 465   C. 299

---

8. Compare these numbers. Make the number sentence true.

   789 ◯ 7,089

   A. >   B. =   C. <

---

9. What number is **100 less**?

   651

   A. 650   B. 615   C. 551

---

10. What number is **100 more**?

    2,703

    A. 2,713   B. 3,703   C. 2,803

---

11. Add.

    ```
      356
    + 403
    ─────
    ```

    A. 759   B. 760   C. 750

---

12. Subtract.

    ```
      878
    - 342
    ─────
    ```

    A. 665   B. 536   C. 466

KE-804036 © Key Education — Specific Skills: Place Value

Place Value for Parents

Dear Parents and Guardians,

In math class, your child will be learning about place value (ones, tens, and hundreds) and comparing number quantities up to 1,000. The concept of place value is sometimes difficult for children to grasp. To help your child at home, please consider reading the following books and practicing the included activities together with your child:

How Much, How Many, How Far, How Heavy, How Long, How Tall Is 1000? by Helen Nolan and illustrated by Tracy Walker (Kids Can Press, 1995). This delightful story will entertain children with fascinating examples of the quantity of 1000 and encourage them to think about what that number means in different situations. Activity ideas are also included.

MathStart©: Shark Swimathon by Stuart J. Murphy and illustrated by Lynne Cravath (HarperCollins, 2001). The clever use of illustrations shows the reader how to regroup numbers while learning if the sharks can attend swim camp. Additional activity suggestions are also included in the book. This is an excellent book to help your child understand subtraction of two-digit numbers.

Activity: Reading Numbers
Directions: Whenever possible, encourage your child to notice the numbers around him or her. While riding in the car or the city bus, discover with your child the wide array of available examples. Numbers are everywhere! Point out building numbers, speed limit signs, billboards, and license plates. Have your child practice saying the whole number. For example, the license number is not just 7-2-6 QL. It is seven hundred twenty-six or 700 + 20 + 6! Have fun with numbers!

Activity: Practicing Base-Ten Concepts with Cents!
Materials Needed: pennies, dimes, dollars, paper, and pencil
Directions: Encourage your child to work with money by pretending to collect a wage. Use a grid as shown below to add and subtract the money as it is "received" and "spent" (similar to a checkbook register). To keep it simple, disperse your child's "earnings" in increments of pennies, dimes, and dollars. When appropriate, direct your child to exchange 10 pennies for a dime, 100 pennies for a dollar bill, and 10 dimes for a dollar bill. This will further enhance the understanding of place value.

Hundreds Dollars — 100¢ each	Tens Dimes — 10¢ each	Ones Pennies — 1¢ each

Thank you for your assistance,

Using Manipulatives and Number Charts

Turtle Ten-Frame Grids and Hippo Hundred Grid

Before having the students start working with numbers greater than 300, provide opportunities for them to count actual objects to discover just how large the quantities of 100, 200, and 300 are. During these number experiences, children should be encouraged to make 10 groups of ten (using Turtle Ten-Frame Grids) and then gather them into larger bunches of hundreds. For example, large pasta rings, dried beans, and medium pasta shells can be used as math counters. When a collection of 100 items is formed, you might want to have the children glue those objects on a Hippo Hundred Board (page 10). If 10 teams of children make groupings of 100, the class will have made a model for 1,000!

The amount of space 100 items takes is always fascinating for children. Prior to the lesson, place 100 medium pasta shells in a snack-sized resealable plastic bag. This step can also be repeated for a collection of 100 toothpicks and 100 large pasta rings. Show the children these quantities and have them estimate how many items are in each bag. They may be quite surprised to learn that each bag holds the same amount. By the way, this activity is a great introduction for the book *How Much, How Many, How Far, How Heavy, How Long, How Tall Is 1000?*, which is featured in the Place Value for Parents letter.

Base-Ten Models

When the children have internalized the concept that 10 groups of ten equal 100, then introduce the flat in a base-ten proportional set. If paper models are used, duplicate five copies of the patterns on page 38 and have the children glue large pasta rings on them. Now the child can touch and count the individual "units" to build a solid understanding that the paper ten-strip represents one group of 10 and the large square represents 100.

Use the prepared base-ten paper models to show specific quantities up to 300. Choose a number and direct the children to select the corresponding hundred-grids, ten-frame grids, and individual squares to build that particular number quantity. Repeat this process several times for various numbers.

Number Charts

Photocopy the number charts on pages 11 and 12 and choose from the following activities:

Even Numbers: Demonstrate with actual items how a number that has a 0, 2, 4, 6, or 8 in the ones place is an even number. Distribute the charts to the children. Direct the students to pick out even numbers and color them lightly with blue. Let them color as many even numbers as they want.

Odd Numbers: Discuss how each number that has a 1, 3, 5, 7, or 9 in the ones place is an odd number. Ask the students to help pick out the odd numbers on their charts. Have them color the odd numbers green. Let them color as many odd numbers as they want.

Counting by 10s: Model counting by 10s, starting with any number. Then have the students continue the sequence with you. As the numbers are announced, have the children cover them with large pasta rings (or other small objects) on the number chart to highlight the pattern. Clear the board each time a new sequence is started.

Making Number Charts to 1000: Have the students work with partners. Assign each team a hundreds section, such as the 200s. Direct each pair of students to fill in a copy of the Hippo Hundred Board (page 10) by writing down the assigned numbers, such as 201–300. When everyone is finished, arrange the charts to show the sequence from 1 to 1000. (Note: If the boxes on the grid are too small for your students, enlarge the copies before distributing them.)

Turtle Ten-Frame Grids

Directions on page 8

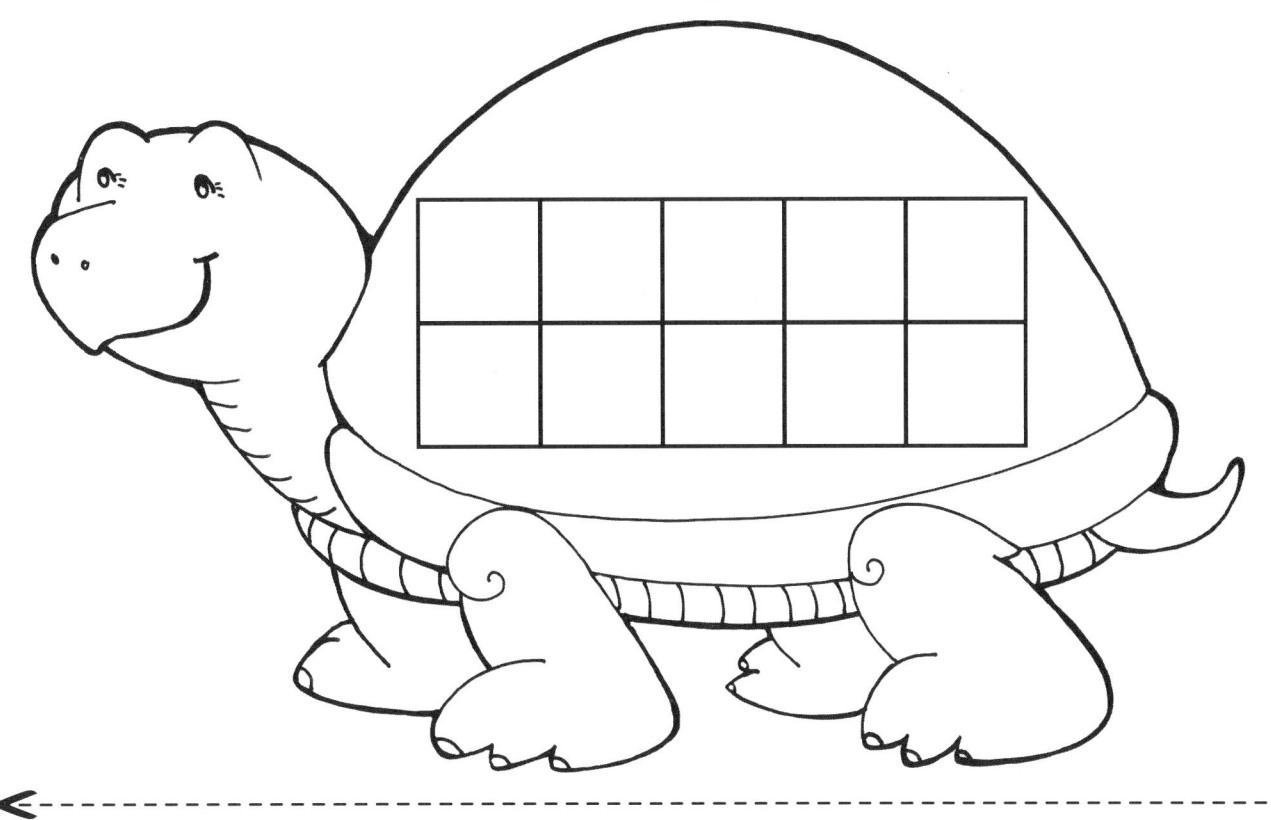

Hippo Hundred Board

Directions on page 8

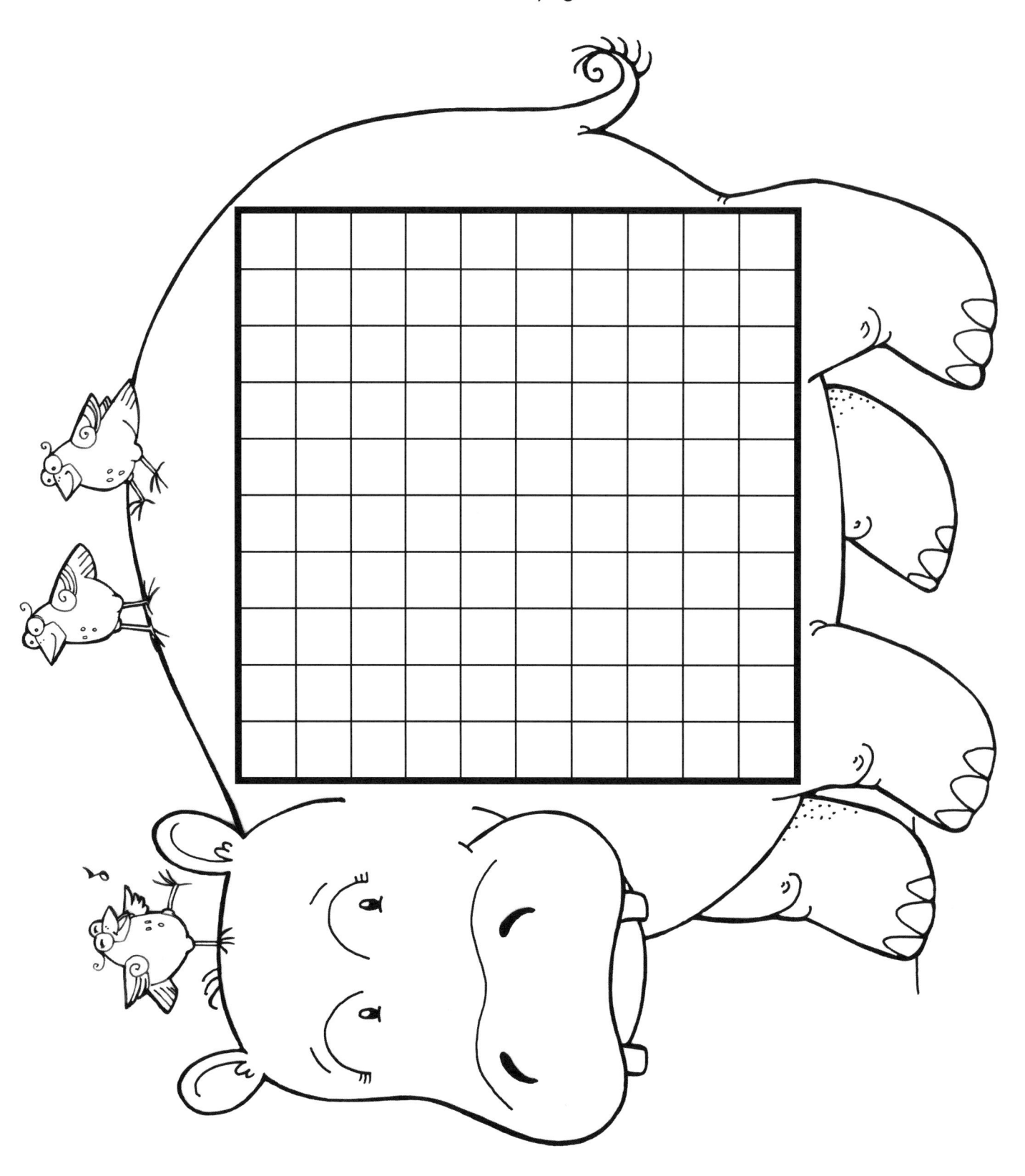

KE-804036 © Key Education — 10 — *Specific Skills: Place Value*

Number Charts

1 to 100

1	2	3	4	5	6	7	8	9	10
11	12	13	14	15	16	17	18	19	20
21	22	23	24	25	26	27	28	29	30
31	32	33	34	35	36	37	38	39	40
41	42	43	44	45	46	47	48	49	50
51	52	53	54	55	56	57	58	59	60
61	62	63	64	65	66	67	68	69	70
71	72	73	74	75	76	77	78	79	80
81	82	83	84	85	86	87	88	89	90
91	92	93	94	95	96	97	98	99	100

101 to 200

101	102	103	104	105	106	107	108	109	110
111	112	113	114	115	116	117	118	119	120
121	122	123	124	125	126	127	128	129	130
131	132	133	134	135	136	137	138	139	140
141	142	143	144	145	146	147	148	149	150
151	152	153	154	155	156	157	158	159	160
161	162	163	164	165	166	167	168	169	170
171	172	173	174	175	176	177	178	179	180
181	182	183	184	185	186	187	188	189	190
191	192	193	194	195	196	197	198	199	200

KE-804036 © Key Education

Specific Skills: Place Value

Number Charts

201 to 300

201	202	203	204	205	206	207	208	209	210
211	212	213	214	215	216	217	218	219	220
221	222	223	224	225	226	227	228	229	230
231	232	233	234	235	236	237	238	239	240
241	242	243	244	245	246	247	248	249	250
251	252	253	254	255	256	257	258	259	260
261	262	263	264	265	266	267	268	269	270
271	272	273	274	275	276	277	278	279	280
281	282	283	284	285	286	287	288	289	290
291	292	293	294	295	296	297	298	299	300

301 to 400

301	302	303	304	305	306	307	308	309	310
311	312	313	314	315	316	317	318	319	320
321	322	323	324	325	326	327	328	329	330
331	332	333	334	335	336	337	338	339	340
341	342	343	344	345	346	347	348	349	350
351	352	353	354	355	356	357	358	359	360
361	362	363	364	365	366	367	368	369	370
371	372	373	374	375	376	377	378	379	380
381	382	383	384	385	386	387	388	389	390
391	392	393	394	395	396	397	398	399	400

KE-804036 © Key Education

Specific Skills: Place Value

Name _____   Date _____

Matching Sets

Directions: Each 🐢 is 10. Each ▮ is 10. Count the dots and squares. Match the sets. Draw a line to each match. Write the numbers in the boxes below.

A.

B.

C.

D.

Directions: What number comes next? Count by ones. Fill in the blanks.

A. | 37 |, 38 , ____ , ____ , ____

B. | ☐ |, ____ , ____ , ____ , ____

C. | ☐ |, ____ , ____ , ____ , ____

D. | ☐ |, ____ , ____ , ____ , ____

KE-804036 © Key Education — 13 — Specific Skills: Place Value

Name _____   Date _____

Tens and Ones

Directions: Look for groupings of 10 squares. Count by 10s. How many squares are left over for the ones place? Fill in each chart. Write the number.

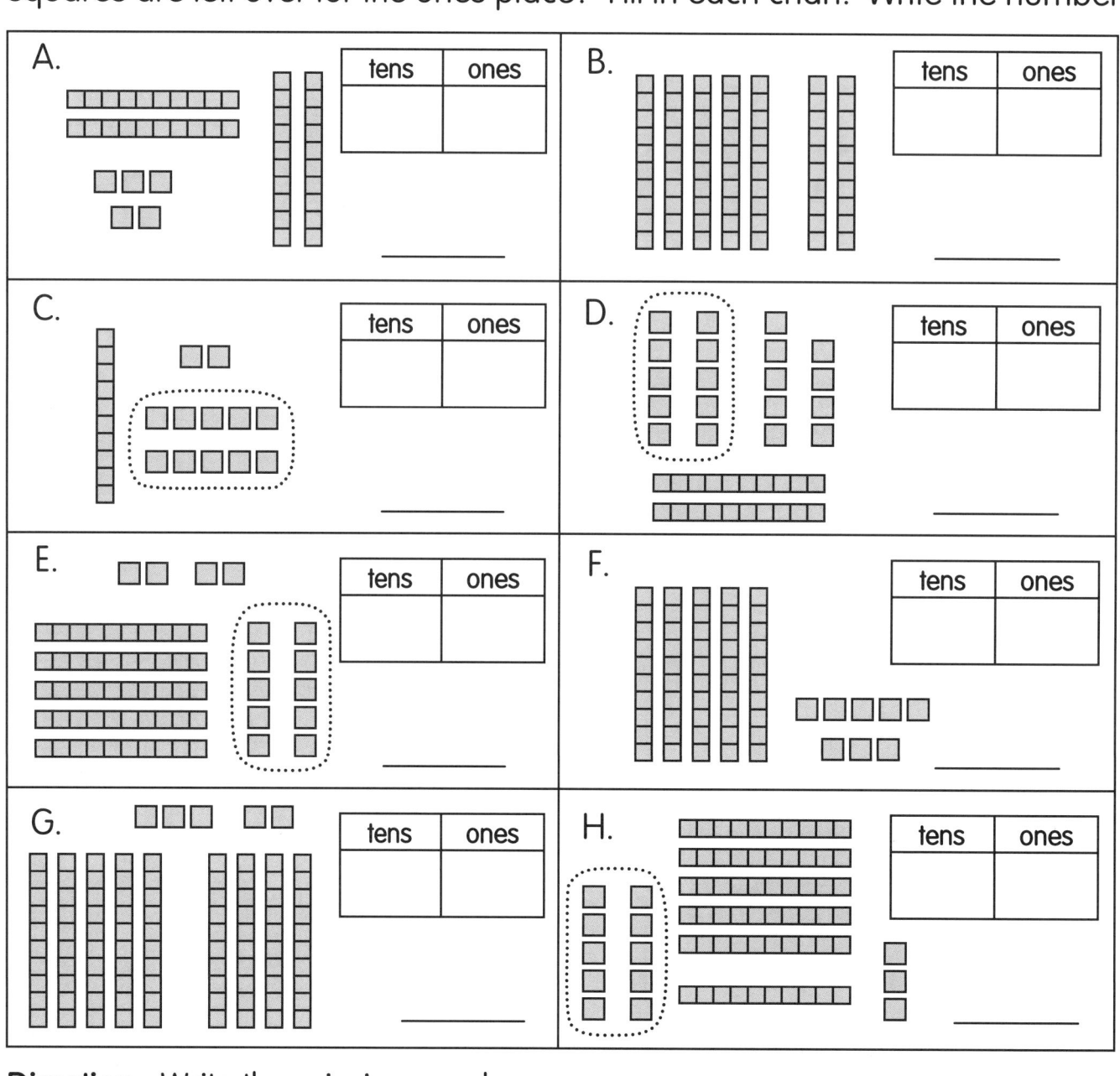

A. | tens | ones |
   |------|------|
   | | |

B. | tens | ones |
   |------|------|
   | | |

C. | tens | ones |
   |------|------|
   | | |

D. | tens | ones |
   |------|------|
   | | |

E. | tens | ones |
   |------|------|
   | | |

F. | tens | ones |
   |------|------|
   | | |

G. | tens | ones |
   |------|------|
   | | |

H. | tens | ones |
   |------|------|
   | | |

Direction: Write the missing numbers.

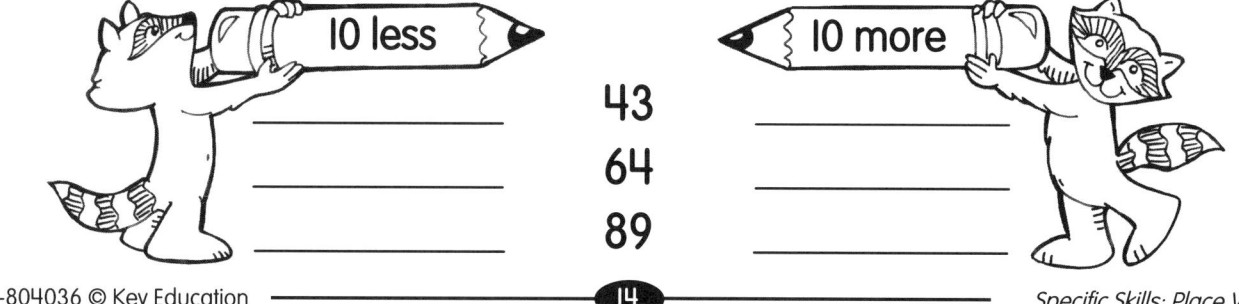

10 less		10 more
_____	43	_____
_____	64	_____
_____	89	_____

KE-804036 © Key Education   Specific Skills: Place Value

Name _____   Date _____

Drivers, Find Your Cars!

Directions: Match each number with its **expanded form** on the car. Write the letter in the blank.

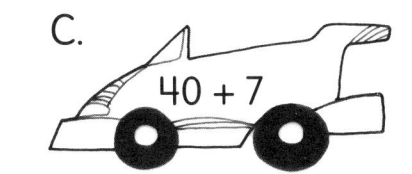

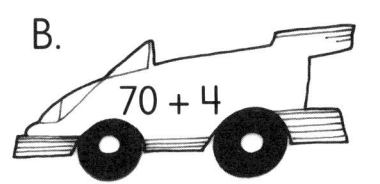

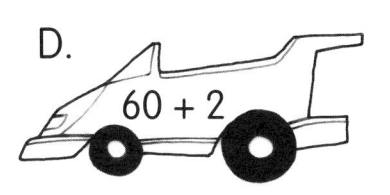

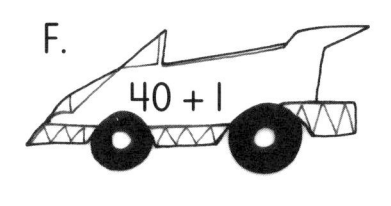

Example: 34   =   30 + 4

A.   50 + 8

B.   70 + 4

C.   40 + 7

D.   60 + 2

E.   80 + 5

F.   40 + 1

G.   20 + 6

H.   90 + 5

1. 41 _____
2. 26 _____
3. 58 _____
4. 62 _____
5. 47 _____
6. 95 _____
7. 85 _____
8. 74 _____

Directions: Skip count by 10s. Write the numbers.

9. 26, ____, ____, ____, ____, ____, ____

10. 68, ____, ____, ____, ____, ____, ____

11. 49, ____, ____, ____, ____, ____, ____

12. 54, ____, ____, ____, ____, ____, ____

KE-804036 © Key Education — 15 — Specific Skills: Place Value

Name _____   Date _____

Crow About These Numbers!

Directions: Read each clue carefully. Write the number on the scarecrow. Write the expanded form in the blanks.

A.

4 tens
9 ones

_____ + _____

B.

7 ones
8 tens

_____ + _____

C.

7 tens
2 ones

_____ + _____

D.

6 ones
5 tens

_____ + _____

Direction: Write the expanded form for each number given.

E. 65 = _____ + _____   F. 93 = _____ + _____

G. 28 = _____ + _____   H. 31 = _____ + _____

Name _____   Date _____

Is It Odd or Even?

Directions: Show each number. Draw / for tens and dots on the turtle for ones. Decide if the number is **odd** or **even**. Circle the correct word.

A. 43 =   tens   ones    odd / even

B. 36 =   tens   ones    odd / even

C. 51 =   tens   ones    odd / even

Directions: Read each number. Write **odd** or **even** in the blank.

D. 28 _____   K. 77 _____

E. 83 _____   L. 49 _____

F. 96 _____   M. 34 _____

G. 61 _____   N. 52 _____

H. 112 _____   O. 125 _____

I. 127 _____   P. 134 _____

J. 140 _____

KE-804036 © Key Education — 17 — Specific Skills: Place Value

Name _____ Date _____

Greater Than, Less Than, Equal To

Directions: Study the place value models. Write the numbers in the blanks. Use greater than (>), less than (<), or equal to (=) in each circle.

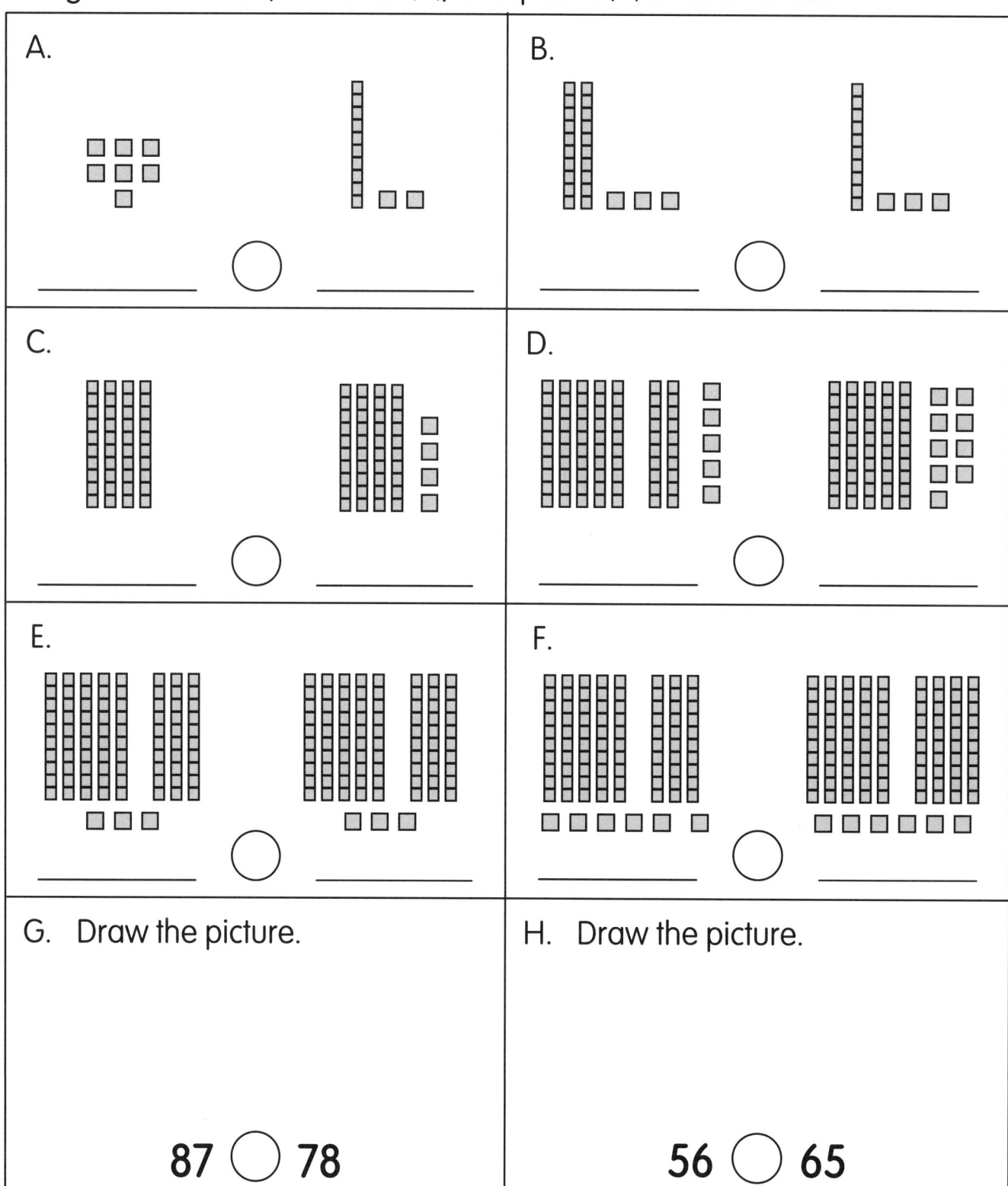

A.

_____ ◯ _____

B.

_____ ◯ _____

C.

_____ ◯ _____

D.

_____ ◯ _____

E.

_____ ◯ _____

F.

_____ ◯ _____

G.   Draw the picture.

87 ◯ 78

H.   Draw the picture.

56 ◯ 65

KE-804036 © Key Education — Specific Skills: Place Value

Name _____   Date _____

Big Fish

Directions: Each fish stands for 100.
Count the fish. Write the numbers on the lines.

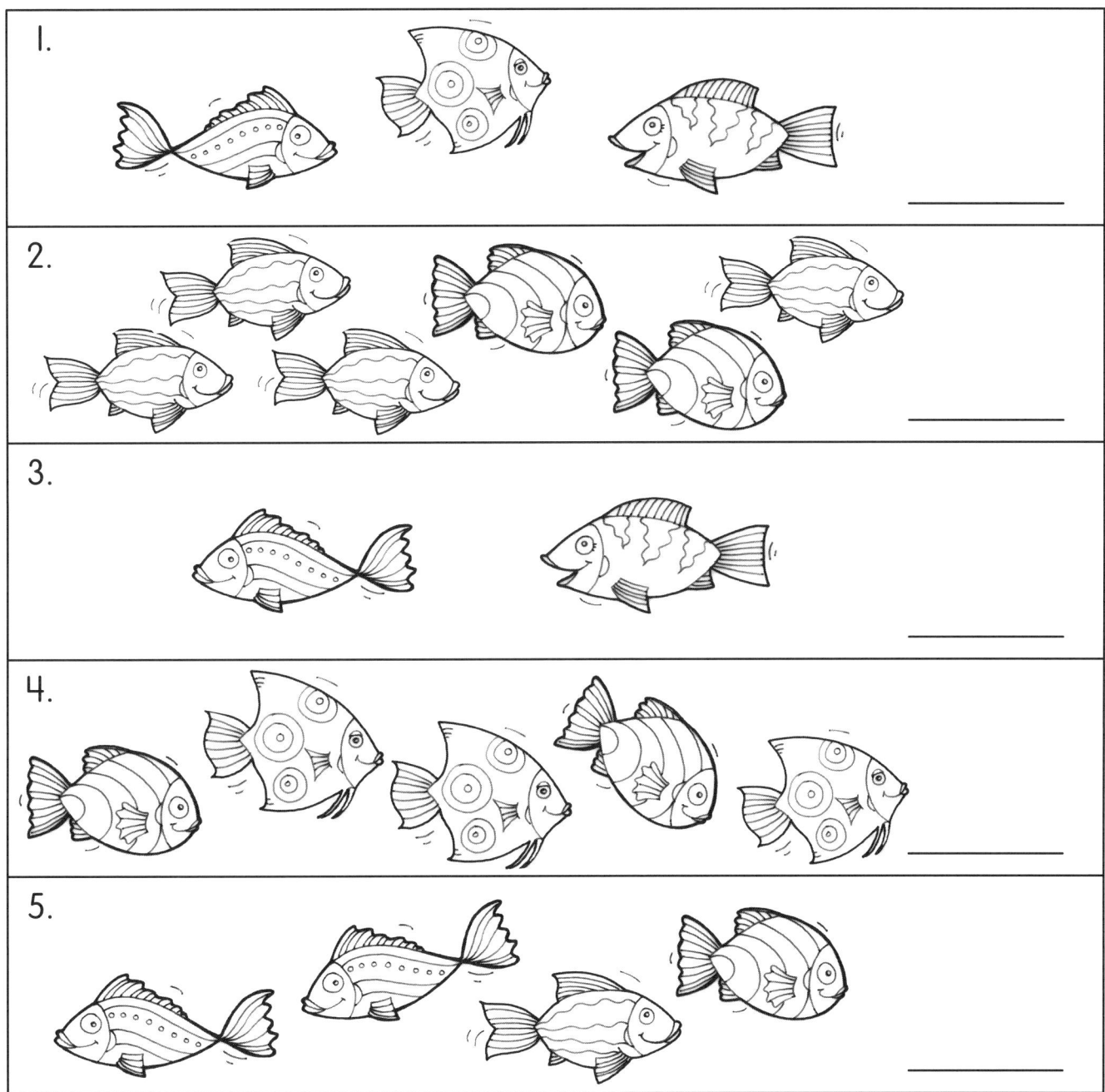

1. _____

2. _____

3. _____

4. _____

5. _____

Directions: Skip count by 100s. Write the missing numbers.

100, ____, ____, ____, ____, ____, ____, ____, ____

KE-804036 © Key Education — 19 — Specific Skills: Place Value

Name _____   Date _____

Cool Counting by 10s

Directions: Count by 10s. Start at 100. Draw lines to connect the dots.

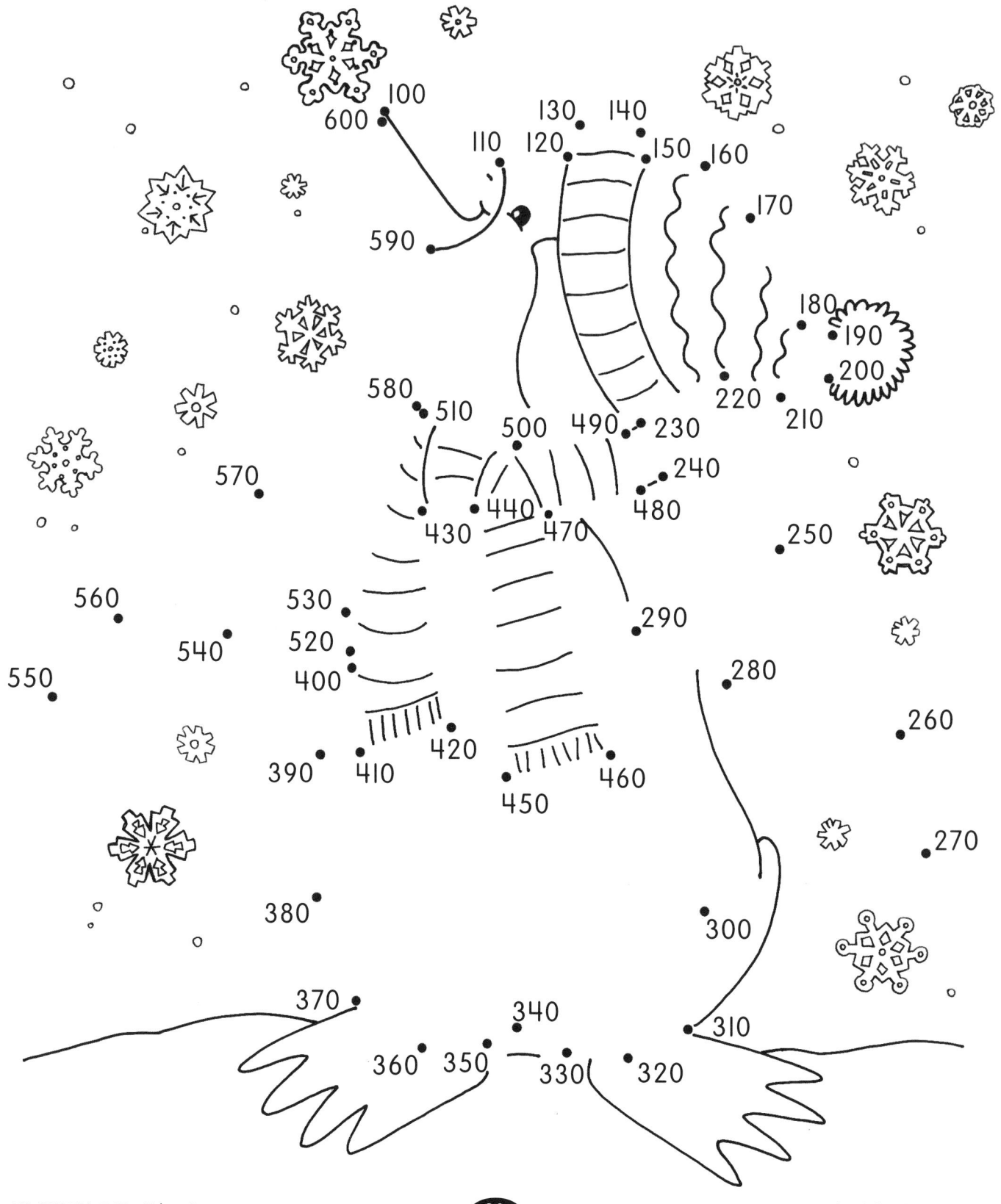

KE-804036 © Key Education — 20 — Specific Skills: Place Value

Name _____ Date _____

Winning Numbers

Directions: Skip count by 20s. Write the numbers in the boxes.

	20		40		60				

Directions: Count backwards by 10s. Write the winning numbers.

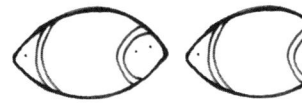

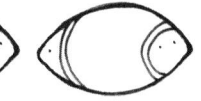

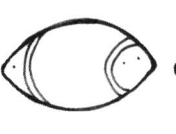

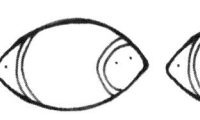

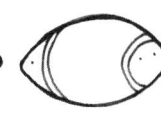

A. 46, 36, ___, ___, ___

B. 72, ___, ___, ___, ___

C. 167, ___, ___, ___, ___

Name _____   Date _____

Taking a Hike!

Directions: Follow the paths. Each ▱ equals 10. Each ▪ equals 1. Count the numbers for each hiker. Write each hiker's number in the box at the end of their path. Circle the hiker who collects the most.

Specific Skills: Place Value

Name _____   Date _____

Counting Hundreds and Tens

Directions: Count the hundreds (▦) and tens (|). Make groupings of 100. How many tens are left over? Fill in the chart. Write the number.

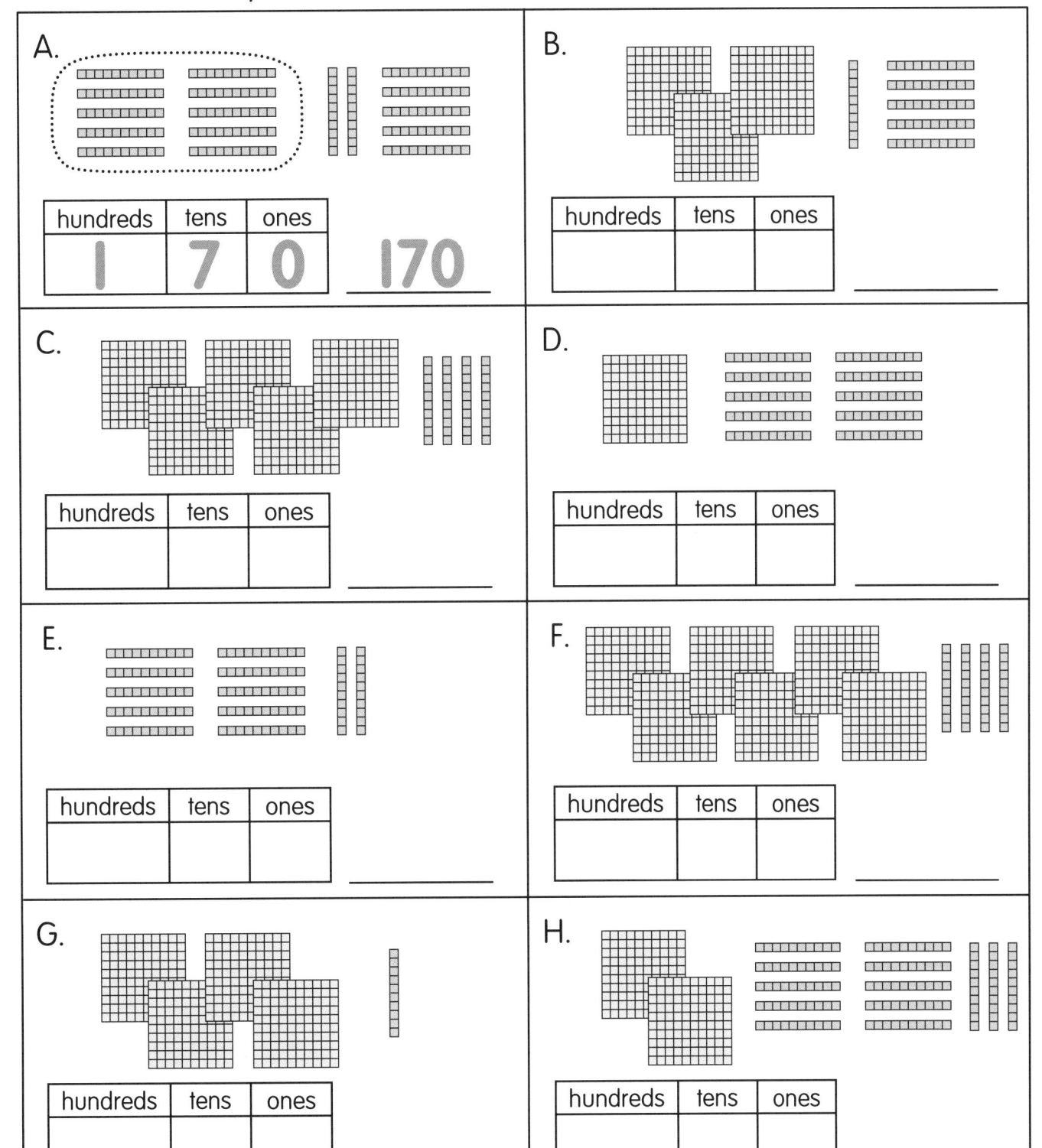

A.

hundreds	tens	ones
1	7	0

170

B.

hundreds	tens	ones

_____

C.

hundreds	tens	ones

_____

D.

hundreds	tens	ones

_____

E.

hundreds	tens	ones

_____

F.

hundreds	tens	ones

_____

G.

hundreds	tens	ones

_____

H.

hundreds	tens	ones

_____

KE-804036 © Key Education — Specific Skills: Place Value

Name _____ Date _____

Charting Hundreds, Tens, and Ones

Directions: Look for groupings of 100 and circle them. Count the hundreds, tens, and ones. Fill in each chart and write the standard numeral on the line.

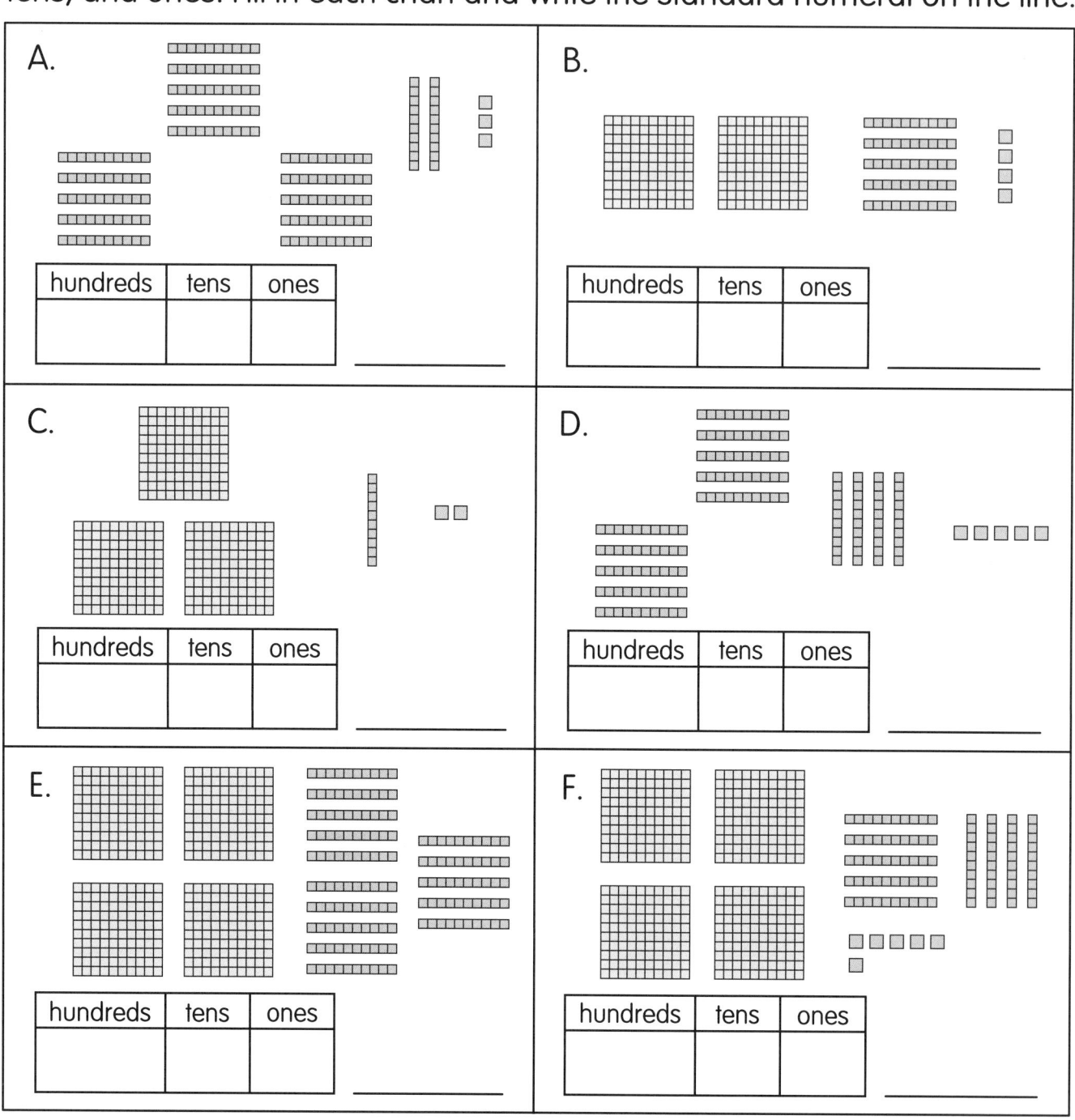

A.

hundreds	tens	ones

B.

hundreds	tens	ones

C.

hundreds	tens	ones

D.

hundreds	tens	ones

E.

hundreds	tens	ones

F.

hundreds	tens	ones

Direction: Write the numbers shown above in order from **greatest** to **least**.

greatest

KE-804036 © Key Education — Specific Skills: Place Value

Name _____ Date _____

Picture These Number Clues!

Directions: Use the picture key below to find out the numbers. Write the numbers on the lines.

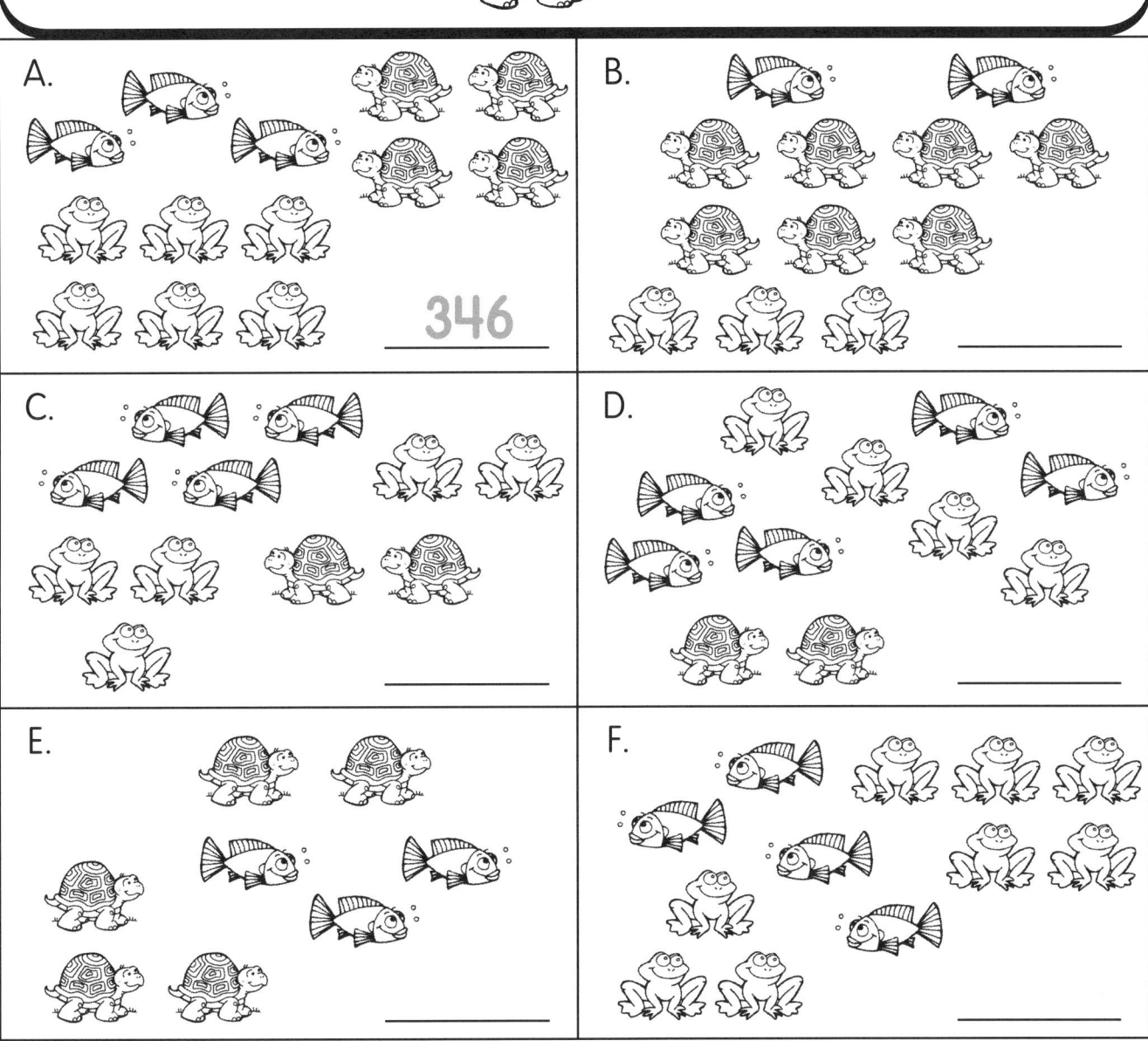

Key

🐟 = 100   🐢 = 10   🐸 = 1

A. _346_

B. _____

C. _____

D. _____

E. _____

F. _____

Directions: Write the numbers shown above in order on the lilly pads.

least _____ _____ _____ _____ _____ _____ greatest

Name _____   Date _____

You Make the Picture!

Directions: Draw a picture for each place value in the key. Use your key when drawing pictures for the numbers.

My Picture Key	hundreds	tens	ones

A.

hundreds	tens	ones
2	5	8

B.

hundreds	tens	ones
4	0	7

C.

hundreds	tens	ones
1	6	5

D.

hundreds	tens	ones
3	7	9

E.

hundreds	tens	ones
5	1	4

KE-804036 © Key Education — Specific Skills: Place Value

Name _____ Date _____

Sidewalk Block Math

Directions: Circle to make groups of 100. Add and write the total.

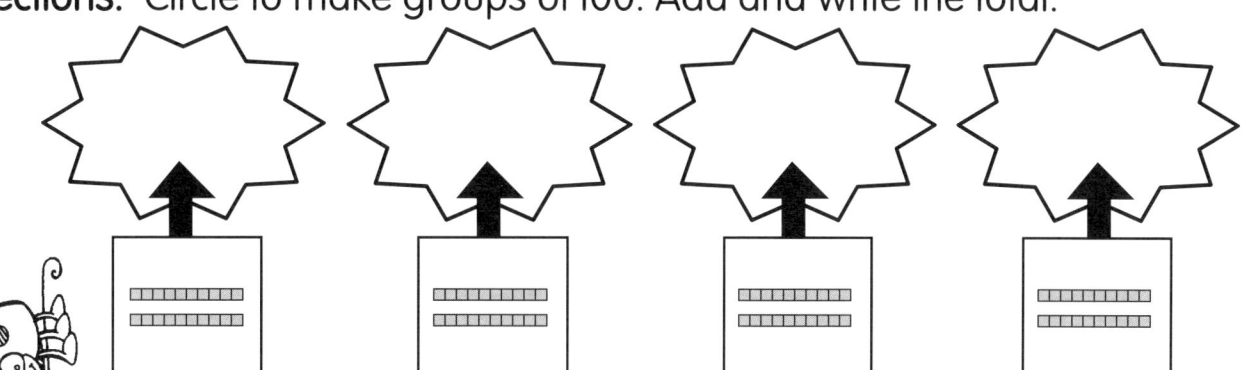

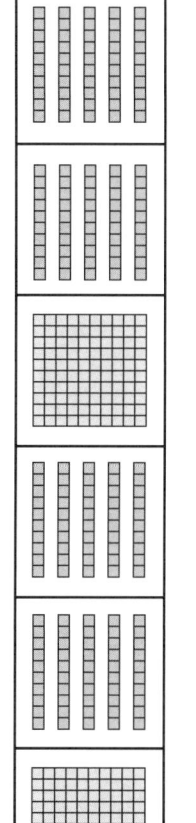

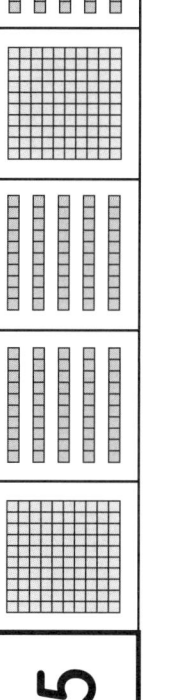

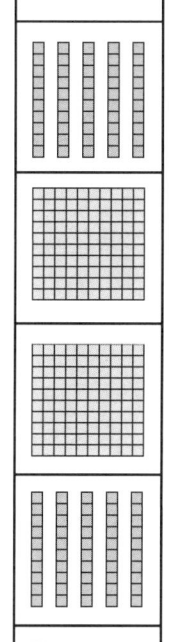

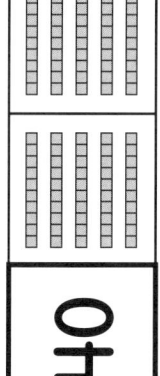

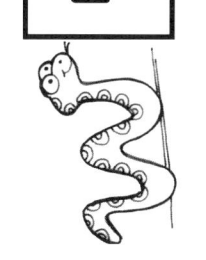

Remember: Each ▦ equals 100. Each ▊ equals 10.

| 60 | 55 | 40 | 37 |

Specific Skills: Place Value

Name _____   Date _____

Riddle My Numbers

Directions: Read the number word. Write the standard form on the line. Use the letter under each answer to solve the riddle.

1. seventeen ___ T	2. thirty-three ___ Y	3. sixty-seven ___ L
4. ninety-one ___ I	5. one hundred twenty ___ C	6. two hundred forty-four ___ U
7. three hundred thirty-eight ___ F	8. five hundred six ___ E	9. six hundred fifty-two ___ O

10. eight hundred seventy-five

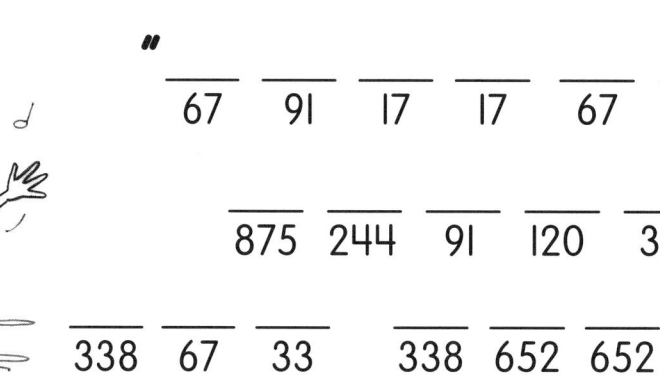

___
J

Riddle: What is a frog's favorite song?

"___ ___ ___ ___ ___ ___
 67   91   17   17   67 506

___ ___ ___ ___ ___
875 244 91 120 33

___ ___ ___ ___ ___ ___ ..."
338 67   33   338 652 652

Name _____   Date _____

What Comes Before or After?

Directions: Write the missing number that comes before each series of numbers.

A. ___, 24, 25	B. ___, 40, 41	C. ___, 68, 69
D. ___, 181, 182	E. ___, 201, 202	F. ___, 356, 357

111 112 113 114 115   116 117 118 119 120

Directions: Count by ones. What comes after? Write the missing numbers.

G. 36, 37, ___, ___	H. 48, 49, ___, ___	I. 173, 174, ___, ___
J. 198, 199, ___, ___	K. 209, ___, ___	L. 459, ___, ___
M. 688, ___, ___	N. 799, ___, ___	O. 909, ___, ___

KE-804036 © Key Education — Specific Skills: Place Value

Name _____ Date _____

Picturing Between Numbers

Directions: Read the numbers. Use the chart to color the picture.

White — 0 to 20	Yellow — 88 to 211
Blue — 21 to 44	Red — 212 to 454
Green — 45 to 62	Orange — 455 to 699
Purple — 63 to 87	Brown — 700 to 999

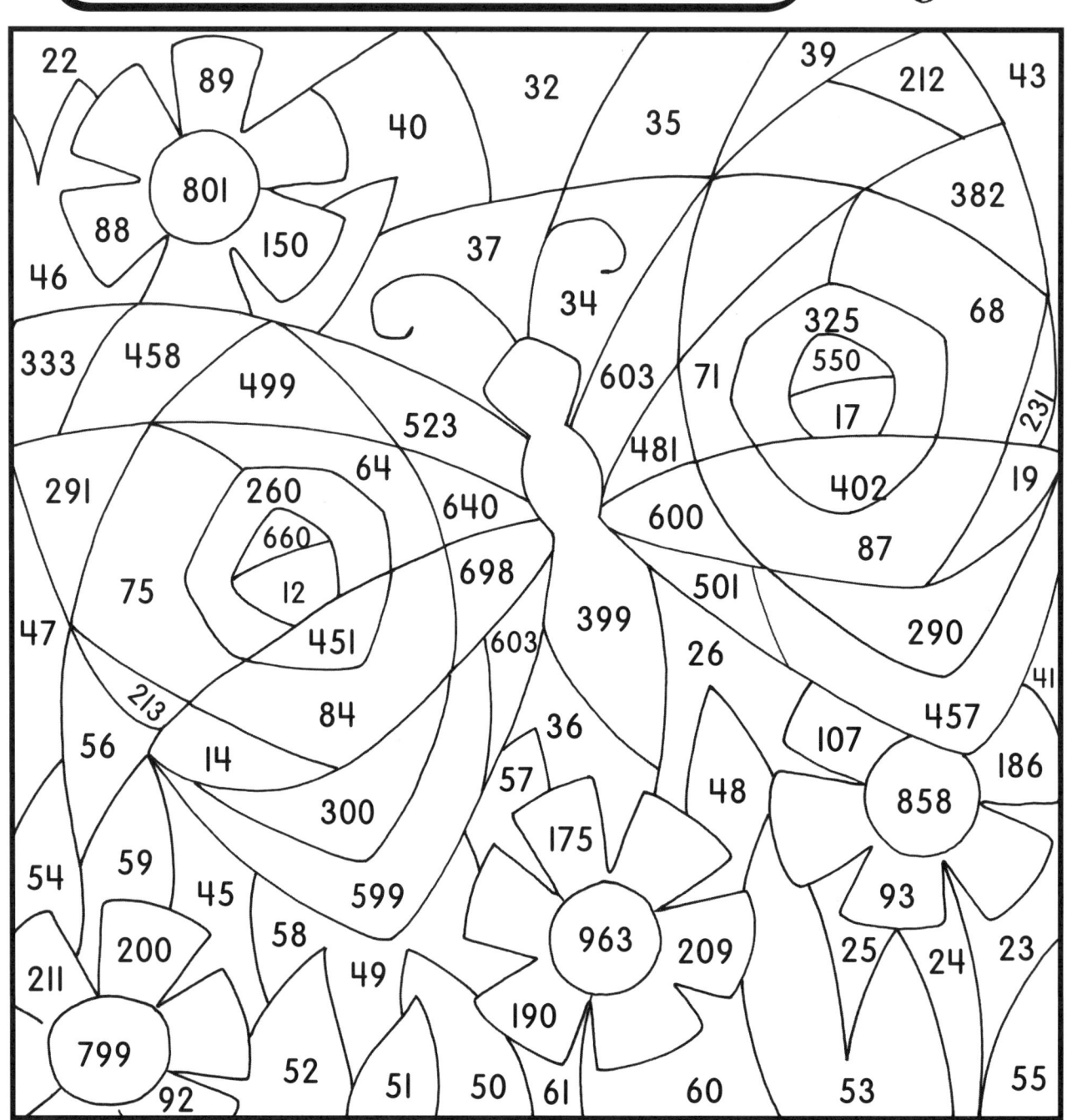

KE-804036 © Key Education

Specific Skills: Place Value

One More Time . . . >, <, or =

Directions: Compare the numbers. Write >, <, or = in each circle.

1. Circle the correct words to complete the sentence:
   The number of flies [578] is (**greater than**, less than, equal to) the number of frogs [187] at the pond.

   578 ◯ 187

2. 103 ◯ 93

3. 222 ◯ 222

4. 289 ◯ 309

5. 343 ◯ 434

6. 568 ◯ 560

7. 582 ◯ 582

8. 614 ◯ 614

9. 706 ◯ 607

10. 747 ◯ 738

11. 846 ◯ 916

12. 977 ◯ 992

Ribbit, Ribbit! Yum!

Name _____   Date _____

Ordering Numbers

Directions: Write the numbers in order from **greatest** to **least**.

A. 48 33 55 55 48 33	B. 179 188 190 _____	C. 252 107 225 _____
D. 500 333 445 _____	E. 628 642 602 _____	F. 924 904 914 _____

Directions: Write the numbers in order from **least** to **greatest**.

G. 178 166 182 _____	H. 91 104 98 _____	I. 266 221 239 _____
J. 403 607 555 _____	K. 699 757 720 _____	L. 831 819 808 _____

KE-804036 © Key Education — Specific Skills: Place Value

Name _____   Date _____

Stretch Out Numbers

Directions: Write each standard number in expanded form on a snake.
For example: 225 = 200 + 20 + 5

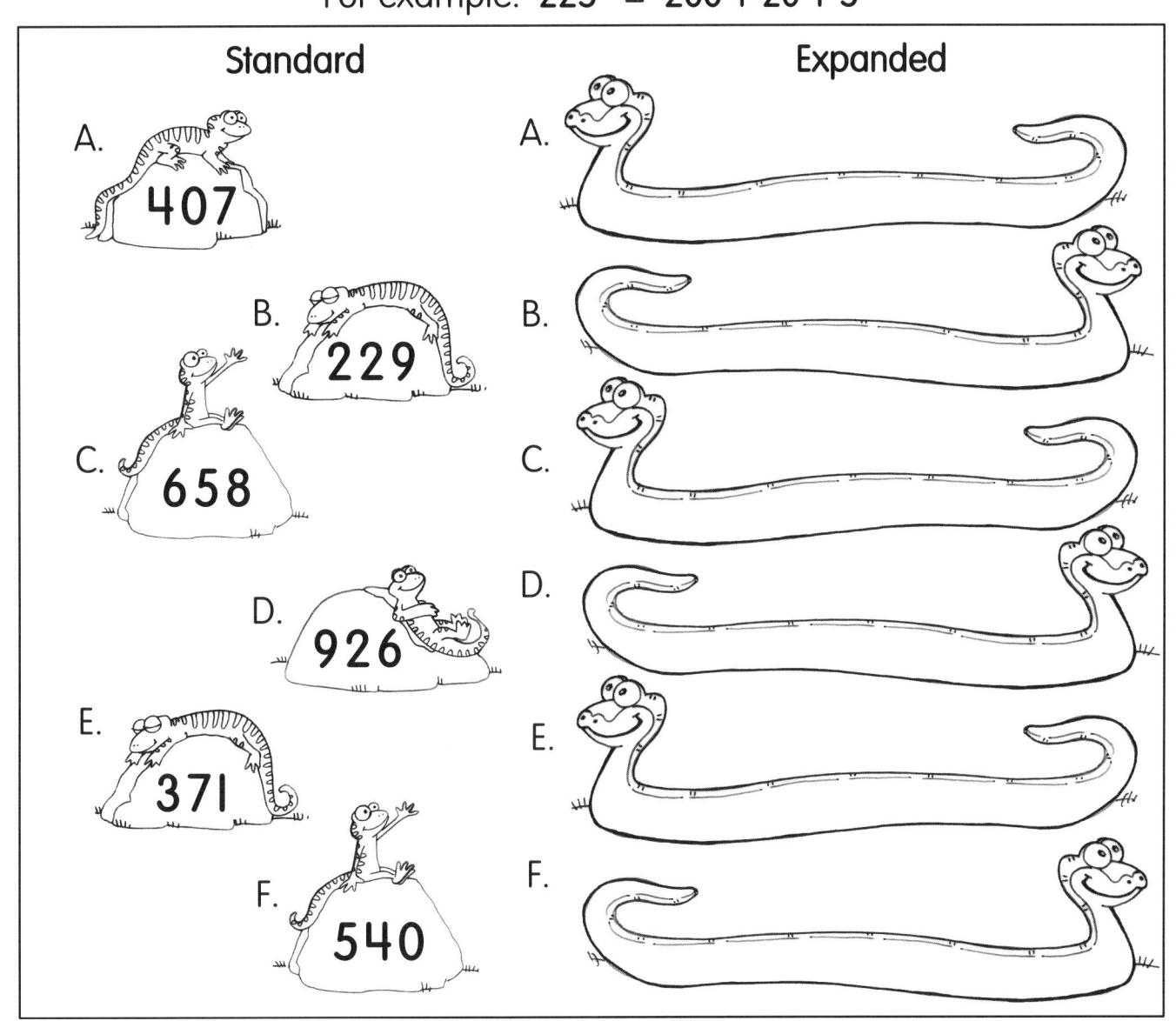

Standard | Expanded

A. 407
B. 229
C. 658
D. 926
E. 371
F. 540

Write It, Expand It!

Directions: Write new numbers between 355 and 975 on the rocks in order. Write the expanded form for the six numbers on the back of this paper.

624

least   greatest

Specific Skills: Place Value

Name _____   Date _____

Snap Up Numbers!

Directions: Read each clue. Write the standard number on the alligator. Write the expanded form in the blanks.

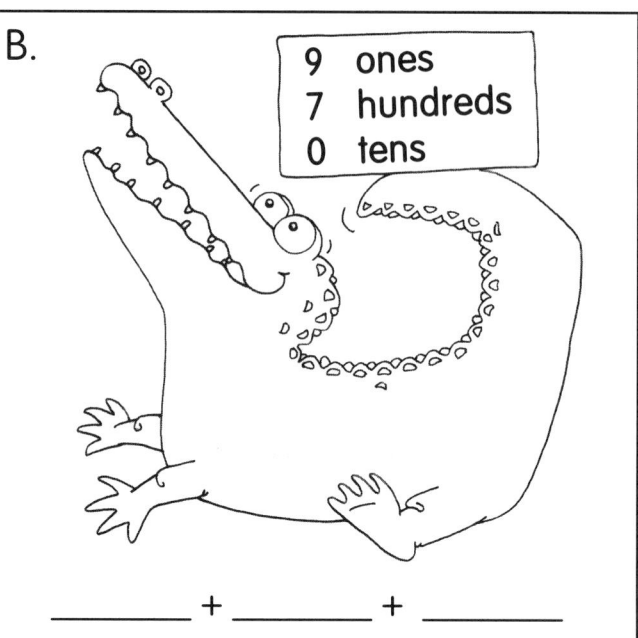

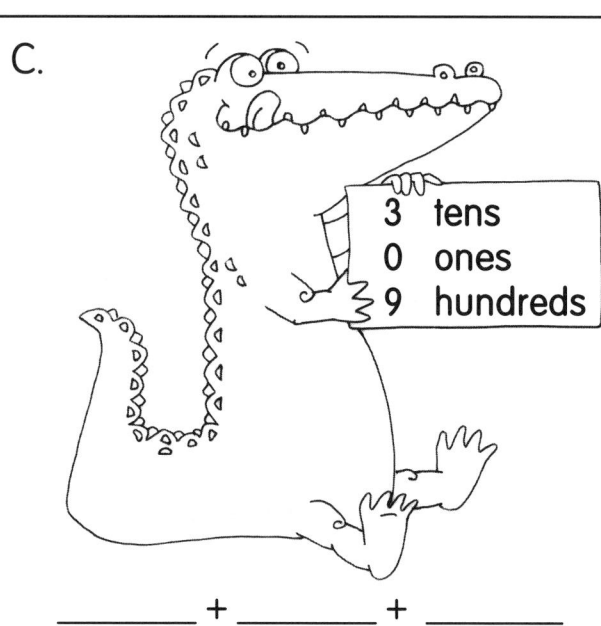

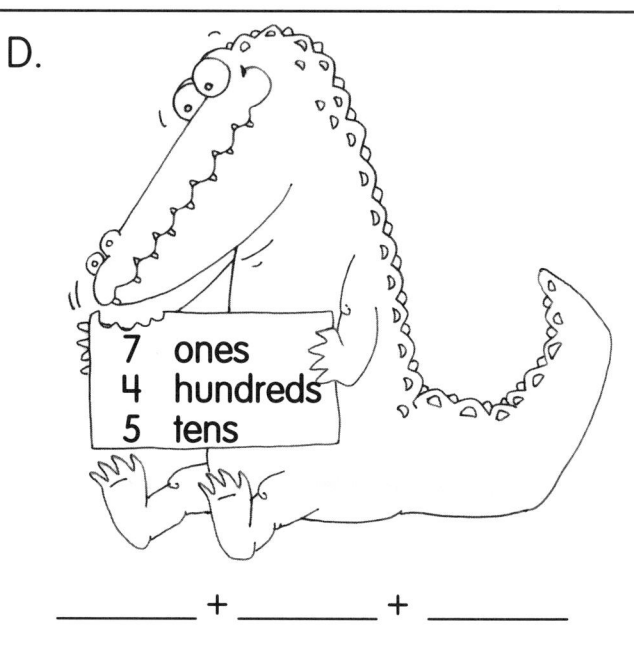

A.
4 tens
2 hundreds
6 ones

_____ + _____ + _____

B.
9 ones
7 hundreds
0 tens

_____ + _____ + _____

C.
3 tens
0 ones
9 hundreds

_____ + _____ + _____

D.
7 ones
4 hundreds
5 tens

_____ + _____ + _____

Direction: Write the expanded form for each number given.

E.   185 = _____ + _____ + _____

F.   560 = _____ + _____ + _____

G.   402 = _____ + _____ + _____

H.   627 = _____ + _____ + _____

KE-804036 © Key Education

Specific Skills: Place Value

Name _____   Date _____

Less and More

Directions: Write the missing numbers on the lines.

10 Less   10 More

A. _____ 14 _____

B. _____ 95 _____

C. _____ 105 _____

D. _____ 255 _____

E. _____ 903 _____

50 Less   50 More

F. _____ 50 _____

G. _____ 100 _____

H. _____ 250 _____

I. _____ 400 _____

J. _____ 650 _____

100 Less   100 More

K. _____ 100 _____

L. _____ 307 _____

M. _____ 562 _____

N. _____ 729 _____

O. _____ 813 _____

P. _____ 603 _____

Q. _____ 884 _____

KE-804036 © Key Education   Specific Skills: Place Value

Name _____   Date _____

Where Is the 4?

Directions: Read each number. Tell if the **4** is in the **ones place**, the **tens place**, or the **hundreds place**.

A. 403 _____	B. 47 _____	C. 114 _____
D. 240 _____	E. 426 _____	F. 94 _____
G. 734 _____	H. 541 _____	

Directions: Give the written form for each number.

I. 283   two hundred eighty-three

J. 167   _____

K. 351   _____

L. 609   _____

M. 840   _____

N. 475   _____

Name _____   Date _____

And the Number Is . . .

Directions: Read each clue. Pick the correct number from the hat and write it on the line.

1. Which number has a 1 in the ones place? _____

2. Which 2 numbers have digits that add up to 9? _____ and _____

3. Which number has the same digit in both the ones and the tens places? _____

4. Which number has no tens **and** no ones? _____

5. In which number is the digit in the tens place **6 less** than the digit in the ones place? _____

6. Which number is **50 more** than 515? _____

7. Which number is **100 less** than 152? _____

8. Which number would come between 801 and 999? _____

9. Which number is missing?

    199, 201, _____, 205, 207

52   565   90
914   36   381   77
800   128   203

Base-Ten Model Patterns

To the teacher: Reproduce these patterns onto card stock and make five copies of this page for each student. Have the students cut apart the pieces. If interested, provide a resealable plastic bag for storing each set of pieces so the students may keep these manipulatives at their desks.

KE-804036 © Key Education — Specific Skills: Place Value

Name _____   Date _____

Hands-On Addition

Directions: Use base-ten models to solve these problems. Write the answers in standard form.

	A. 8 tens 2 ones plus 1 ten 6 ones = _____
B. 1 hundred 2 tens plus 5 tens 9 ones = _____	C. 1 hundreds 4 tens 1 one plus 2 hundreds 5 tens 2 ones = _____
D. 2 hundreds 7 tens 5 ones plus 1 hundred 3 ones = _____	E. 3 hundreds 6 tens 7 ones plus 3 tens = _____
F. 3 hundreds 1 ten 6 ones plus 1 hundred 2 tens 2 ones = _____	G. 4 hundreds 2 tens 1 one plus 2 hundreds 3 tens 1 one = _____

KE-804036 © Key Education — 39 — Specific Skills: Place Value

Name _____   Date _____

Adding with Place Value Chart

Directions: Solve each problem.

1.
hundreds	tens	ones
	1	7
+	3	1

2.
hundreds	tens	ones
9	6	7
+	3	0

3.
hundreds	tens	ones
3	8	5
+ 1	0	4

4.
hundreds	tens	ones
5	3	4
+ 1	1	5

5.
hundreds	tens	ones
1	5	3
+ 4	4	4

6.
hundreds	tens	ones
6	6	4
+ 2	0	2

7.
hundreds	tens	ones
2	8	0
+ 5	1	8

8.
hundreds	tens	ones
7	0	9
+ 2	7	0

9.
hundreds	tens	ones
4	7	1
+ 2	1	6

Name _____   Date _____

Adding with Regrouping

Directions: Add the problems. Regrouping will be necessary.

Example:

hundreds	tens	ones
[1]	[1]	
3	7	8
+ 1	2	4
5	0	2

1. Add the ones column. You must regroup since 8 + 4 = 12.
2. Add the tens column. (1 + 7 + 2 = 10) Regroup!
3. Add the hundreds column. (1 + 3 + 1 = 5)

1.

hundreds	tens	ones
☐	☐	
4	7	0
+	5	5

2.

hundreds	tens	ones
☐	☐	
1	4	3
+ 2	7	0

3.

hundreds	tens	ones
☐	☐	
3	3	9
+ 2	4	6

4.

hundreds	tens	ones
☐	☐	
4	4	4
+ 3	0	8

5.

hundreds	tens	ones
☐	☐	
5	6	3
+ 2	8	7

6.

hundreds	tens	ones
☐	☐	
7	2	9
+ 1	8	8

KE-804036 © Key Education

Specific Skills: Place Value

Name _____   Date _____

Hands-On Subtraction

Directions: Use base-ten models to solve these problems. Write the answers in standard form.

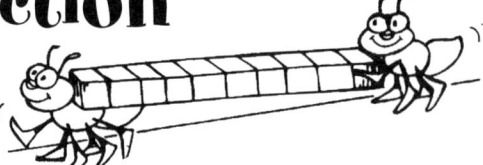

A.	2 hundreds 4 tens 8 ones	minus	5 ones = _____
B.	3 hundreds 5 tens 7 ones	minus	3 tens 3 ones = _____
C.	1 hundred 2 tens 0 ones	minus	1 hundred 1 ten = _____
D.	5 hundreds 6 tens 9 ones	minus	2 hundreds 4 tens = _____
E.	6 hundreds 3 tens 5 ones	minus	1 hundred 2 tens 3 ones = _____
F.	4 hundreds 7 tens 6 ones	minus	3 hundreds 2 ones = _____
G.	6 hundreds 1 ten 4 ones	minus	4 hundreds 4 ones = _____
H.	3 hundreds 3 tens 3 ones	minus	1 hundred 3 tens 3 ones = _____

KE-804036 © Key Education

Specific Skills: Place Value

Name _____   Date _____

Subtracting with Place Value Chart

Directions: Subtract to find the difference.

1.
tens	ones
6	3
− 3	2

2.
tens	ones
8	7
− 5	4

3.
tens	ones
9	7
− 3	1

4.
tens	ones
7	7
− 2	5

5.
hundreds	tens	ones
4	4	2
− 2	1	2

6.
hundreds	tens	ones
7	7	5
− 3	4	4

7.
hundreds	tens	ones
9	8	0
− 4	4	0

8.
hundreds	tens	ones
6	1	6
− 2	1	3

KE-804036 © Key Education   Specific Skills: Place Value

Name _____   Date _____

Subtracting with Regrouping

In each of these problems, regrouping is necessary.
To **regroup** in a subtraction problem, one must borrow.

Example: $\overset{3\ 10}{3\cancel{4}\cancel{0}}$ In the ones column, 5 cannot be subtracted from 0.
             $-\ 2\ 1\ 5$ Move a "10" from the tens column to the ones column
             $\overline{1\ 2\ 5}$ and then subtract. (10 – 5 = 5)

Directions: Solve each problem.

1.
hundreds	tens	ones
☐	☐	☐
3	3	3
−	2	8

2.
hundreds	tens	ones
☐	☐	☐
4	6	3
− 1	2	5

3.
hundreds	tens	ones
☐	☐	☐
3	2	9
−	6	8

4.
hundreds	tens	ones
☐	☐	☐
5	5	7
− 3	2	9

5.
hundreds	tens	ones
☐	☐	☐
6	9	5
− 2	0	6

6.
hundreds	tens	ones
☐	☐	☐
7	4	3
− 5	7	0

Directions for Partner Games

Counting On Logs!

Materials Needed
- game board (page 48)
- game cards (page 47)
- 22 craft sticks, glue, and a box of large pasta rings
- scissors

Getting Ready
- Reproduce the game board onto colored card stock, one per player.
- Duplicate one copy of the game cards onto card stock. Cut the cards apart.
- Glue 10 pasta rings on each craft stick to make 22 "logs" that represent tens. Set aside about 20 pasta rings for individual game pieces.

Objective
Count by 10s from any number

How to Play
Before starting the game, gather the turtle cards and arrange them facedown in a separate area. Place the numeral game cards facedown in the center of the playing area. Set the logs in a pile nearby. Explain to the players that each log equals 10 and that they will be practicing how to count on by 10s from a certain number. For example, 18 plus 10 is 28 and 28 plus 10 equals 38. Provide pencils and paper for keeping track of the scores for each round of play.

To begin, have each player draw a turtle card, read the number, and then place the matching number of logs in the "water" on the game board and pasta rings on the ten-frame grid. Now the players are ready to take turns drawing the numeral game cards (+10, +20, etc.), collecting the matching number of logs, and placing them on their game boards. At the end of each round, the players must figure out the value of the logs (counting by 10s) plus the individual rings and announce their totals correctly to keep the new pieces. If the number is incorrect, that player loses the logs that were just collected. At the end of six rounds of play, the winner is the player who has the highest score.

Alternatively, provide additional +/− number cards and logs. The children can continue the game until 10 rounds of play are completed or until one of the players achieves a predetermined goal, such as the score of 200 or more.

Fly-In 400

Materials Needed
- die pattern (page 47)
- game board pattern (page 49)
- base-ten patterns (page 38)
- scissors and card stock

Getting Ready
- Reproduce a game board for each player. Use colored card stock.
- Duplicate 10 copies of the base-ten pattern page on card stock. Cut apart the pieces.
- Copy one die pattern onto card stock to play the game. Cut out the die shape along the dashed lines. Fold along the solid lines. To make the die, glue the flaps, as indicated, underneath the outer panels to form a cube.

Objective
Count and represent numbers up to 400 with base-ten models

How to Play
Give each player a game board. Place the base-ten paper models (hundred grid, ten-strip pieces, and individual squares) in the center of the playing area. To start the game, have each player roll the die. The player who rolls the largest number begins the first round. The players now take turns rolling the die and collecting the matching number of base-ten pieces. The players may exchange 10 squares for a ten-strip and/or 10 ten-strips for a hundred-grid. At the end of each round the players must announce their totals. If the total is incorrect, that player must put back the game pieces that were just collected. The game ends when the first player reaches a total of 400 to win.

KE-804036 © Key Education — Specific Skills: Place Value

Partner Games Directions

Unlocking the Tens!

Materials Needed
- game patterns (pages 50–52)
- colored file folder
- glue, scissors, and card stock

Getting Ready
- Duplicate and cut out the treasure chests. Glue them on the file folder, four chests on each panel.
- Reproduce the keys and game cards onto card stock. Cut apart the game pieces.

Objectives
Count by 100s from the numbers shown on the treasure chests; find the pairs of two-digit numbers that equal 100 by matching one key with one treasure chest

How to Play
Game A: Place the game cards facedown in a stack in the playing area. Each player chooses three treasure chests on the game board. The players now take turns drawing a card from the pile and deciding if the number shown would be part of the sequence when skip counting by 100s, starting with the numbers represented on the treasure chests. If the card is a match, it is placed under the matching chest. If not, it is returned to the bottom of the draw pile. The first player to collect three cards (nine cards in all) for each selected treasure chest wins the game.

Game B: Each player chooses a panel on the file folder. Scatter the keys facedown in the center of the playing area. To play this game, the players take turns choosing a key and matching it with the corresponding chest to make totals that equal 100. The game ends when all of the pieces have been matched.

Blast Off!

Materials Needed
- game patterns (pages 53 and 54)
- scissors and card stock

Getting Ready
- Reproduce the game board pattern and game cards onto card stock. Cut out the game cards.

Objective
Correctly show the expanded form for numbers up to 999; arrange them in order from greatest to least

How to Play
Place the star cards facedown in a stack and arrange the remaining game pieces faceup. Give each player a game board. Have each player draw a star card. The player who holds the lowest numbered card starts the game by drawing another card and reading the number aloud for the partner. The partner then uses the game pieces to show the expanded form for the selected number. If the player builds the number correctly, that player collects the star card and places it in the top box on their board. If not, the star card is returned to the bottom of the stack. That player now draws a star card to read to the other player who continues the game in the same manner. When a player collects six star cards, that player must quickly arrange them in order from greatest (top) to least (bottom) and shout "Blast Off!" to win the game.

Ten Dollars and Ten Cents

Materials Needed
- game patterns (pages 55 and 56)
- scissors and card stock

Getting Ready
- Make two copies of the game board and game pieces on card stock and cut out the pieces. Make the die according to the directions in Fly-In 400.

Objective
Exchange coins and bills for equivalent amounts

How to Play
Give each player a game board. Place the game pieces and die in the center of the playing area. To start the game have each player roll the die. The player who rolls the largest number begins the first round. The players now take turns rolling the die and collecting the matching amount of money. At the end of each round, the players must announce their new totals. If the total is incorrect, that player must put back the money that was just collected. The game ends when the first player collects $10.10 or more to win.

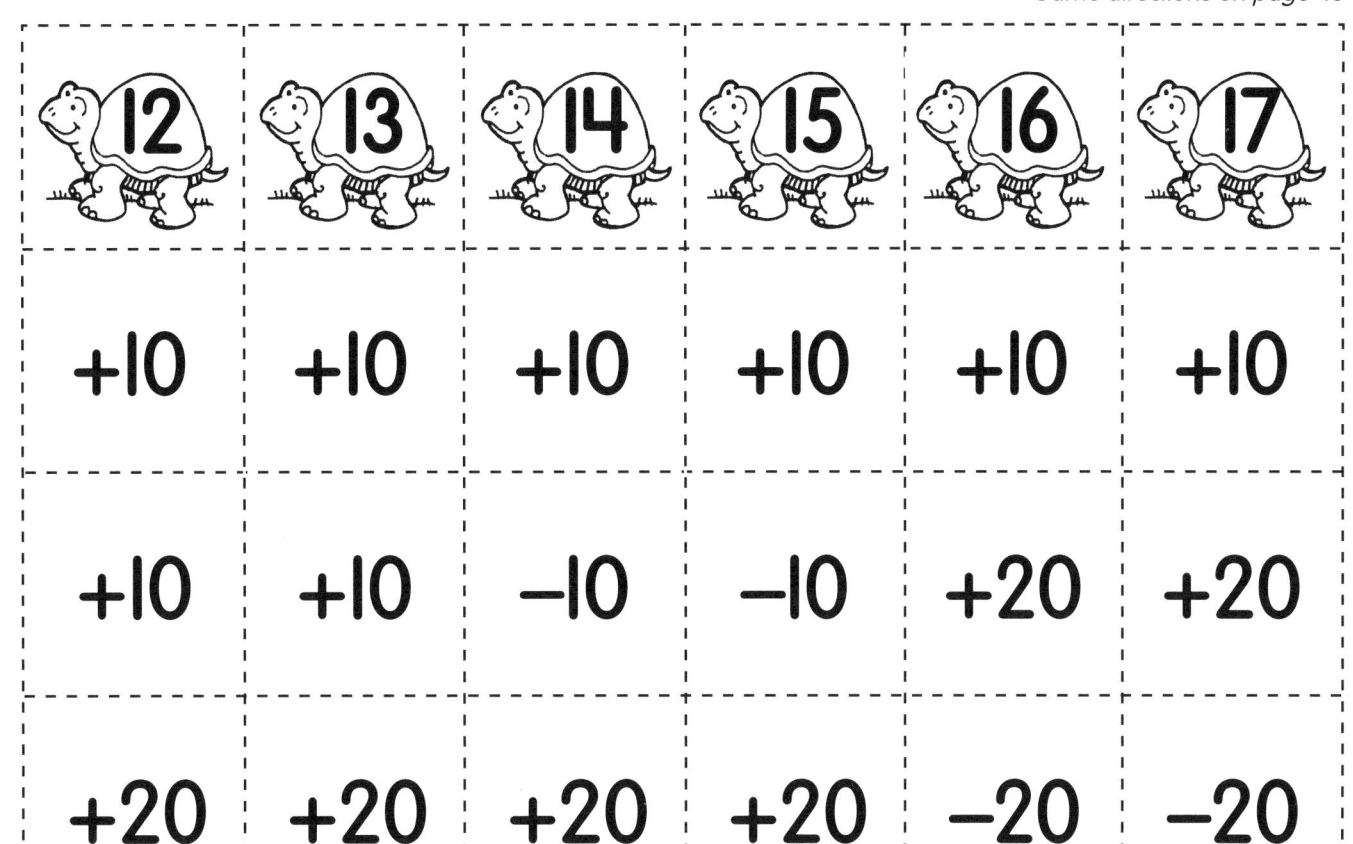

Counting On Logs/Fly-In 400
Game directions on page 45

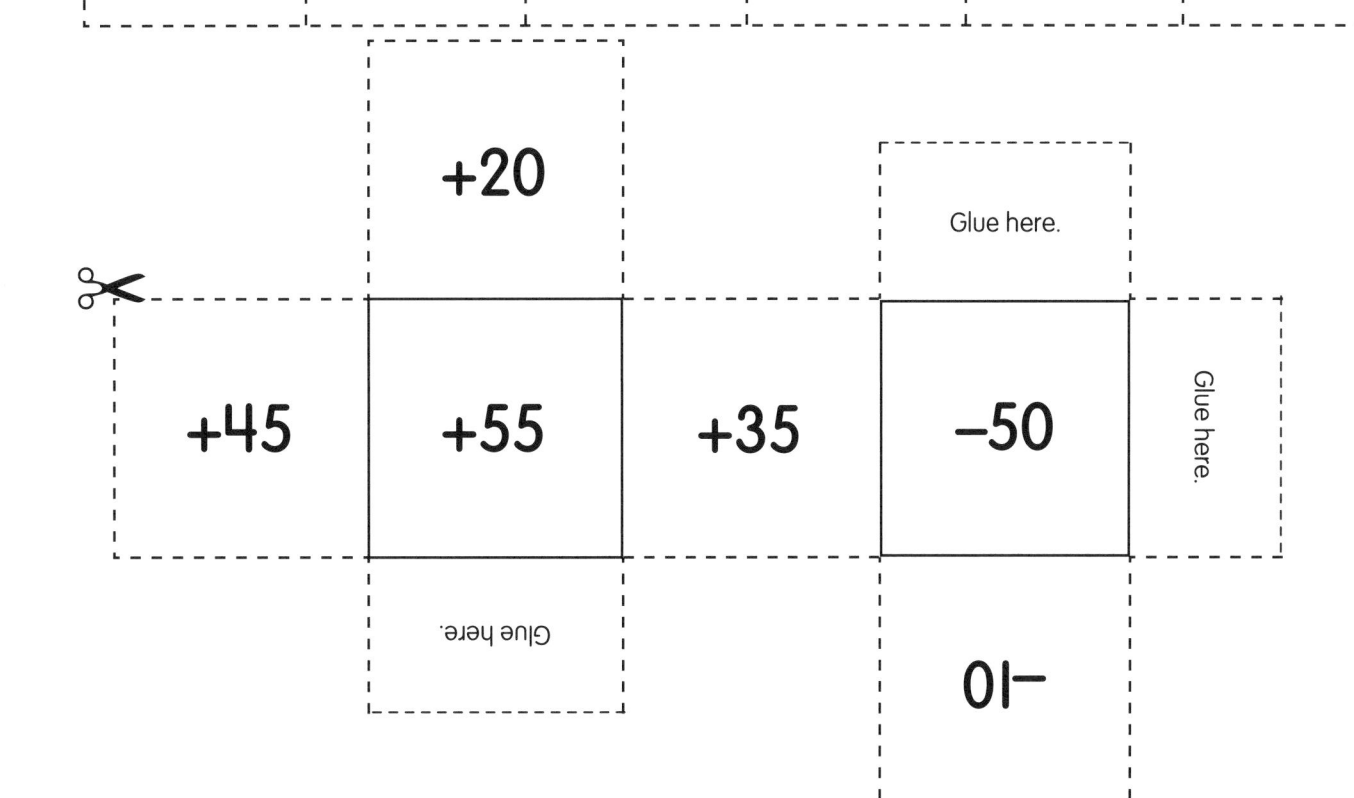

12	13	14	15	16	17
+10	+10	+10	+10	+10	+10
+10	+10	−10	−10	+20	+20
+20	+20	+20	+20	−20	−20

+20

+45 | +55 | +35 | −50 | Glue here.

Glue here.

Glue here.

−10

Specific Skills: Place Value

Counting On Logs

Game directions on page 45

Game directions on page 45

Fly-In 400

hundreds	tens	ones

Specific Skills: Place Value

Unlock the Tens

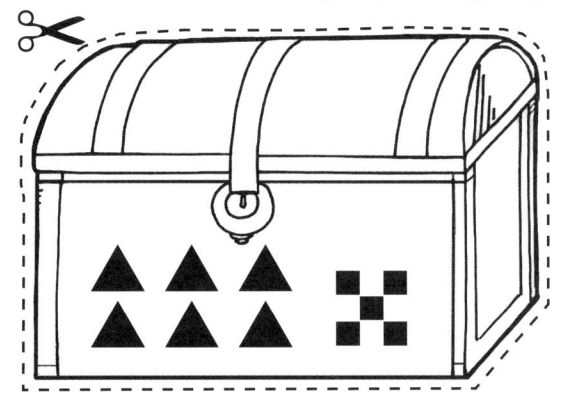

Glue on left panel of file folder

Glue on left panel of file folder

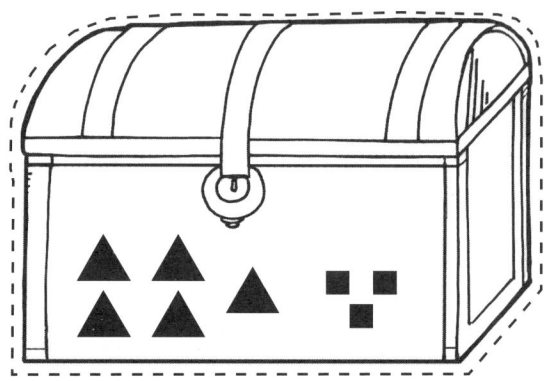

Glue on left panel of file folder

Glue on left panel of file folder

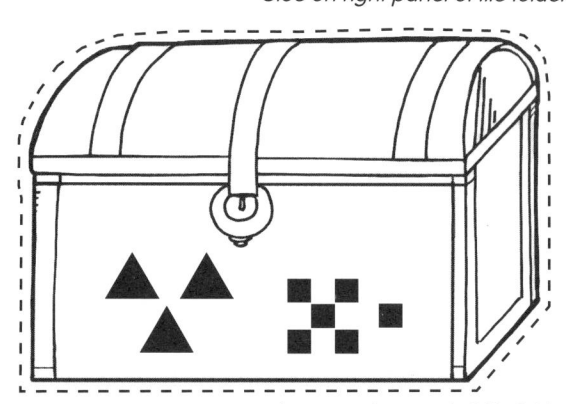

Glue on right panel of file folder

Glue on right panel of file folder

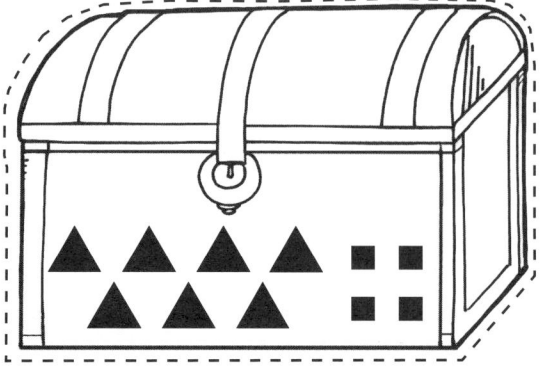

Glue on right panel of file folder

Glue on right panel of file folder

Unlock the Tens — *Label for file folder*

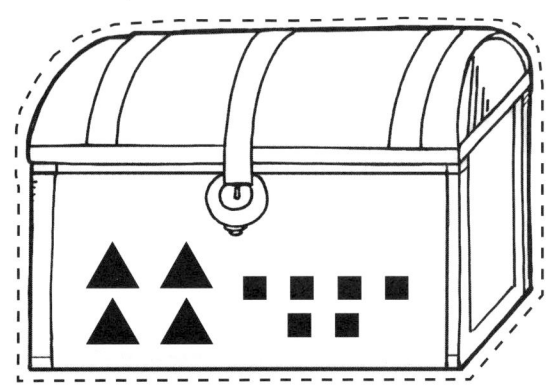

▲ = 10   ■ = 1 — *Key for game board*

Unlock the Tens
Game directions on page 46

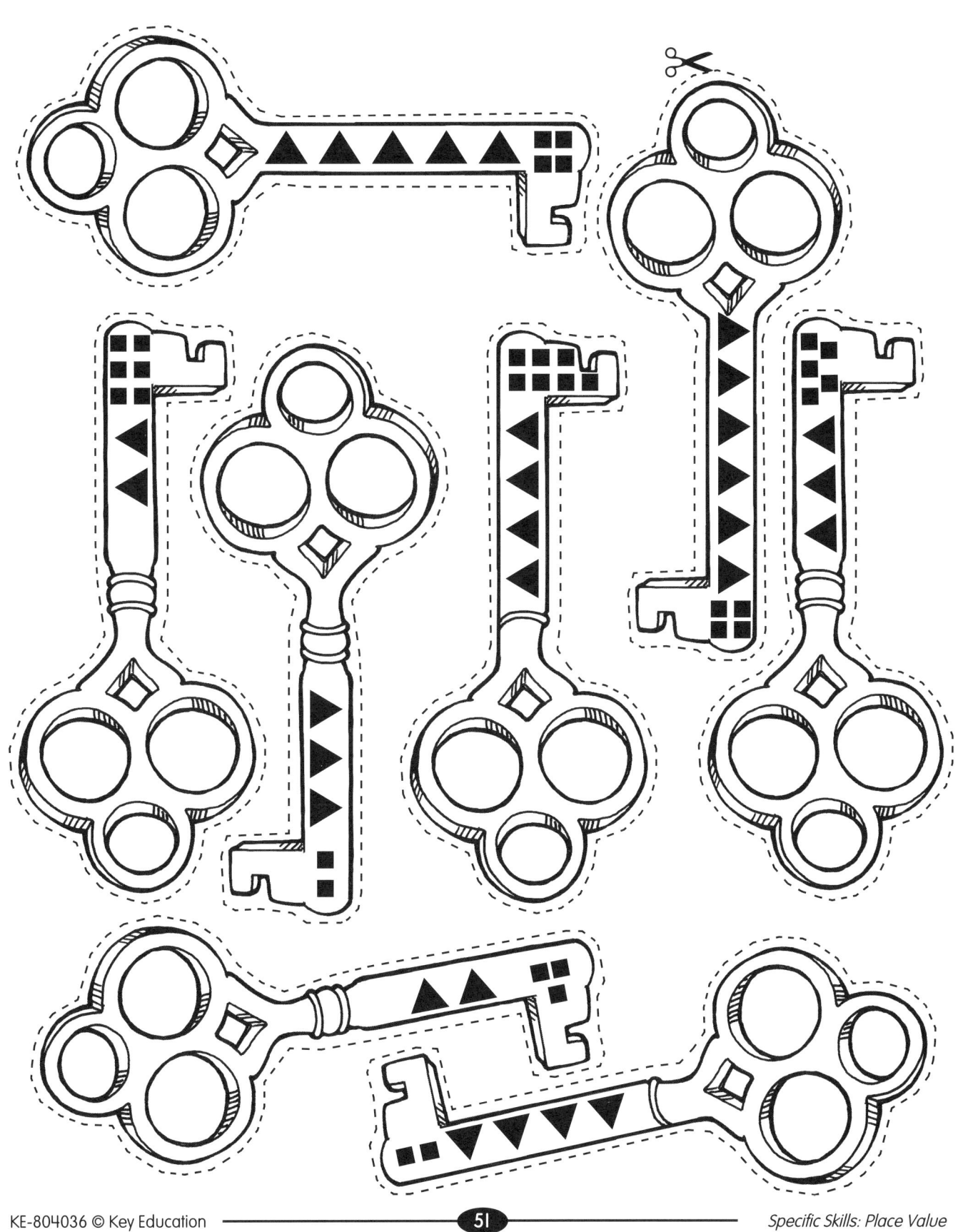

KE-804036 © Key Education — 51 — *Specific Skills: Place Value*

Unlock the Tens
Game directions on page 46

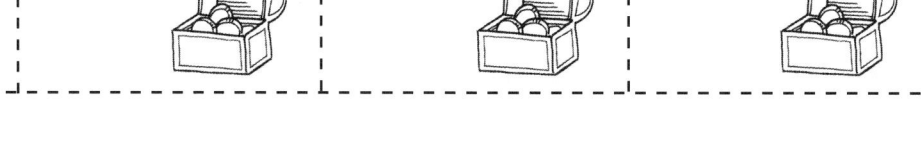

165	146	168	153
158	177	136	174

265	246	268	253
258	277	236	274

365	346	368	353
358	377	336	374

Specific Skills: Place Value

Blast Off!

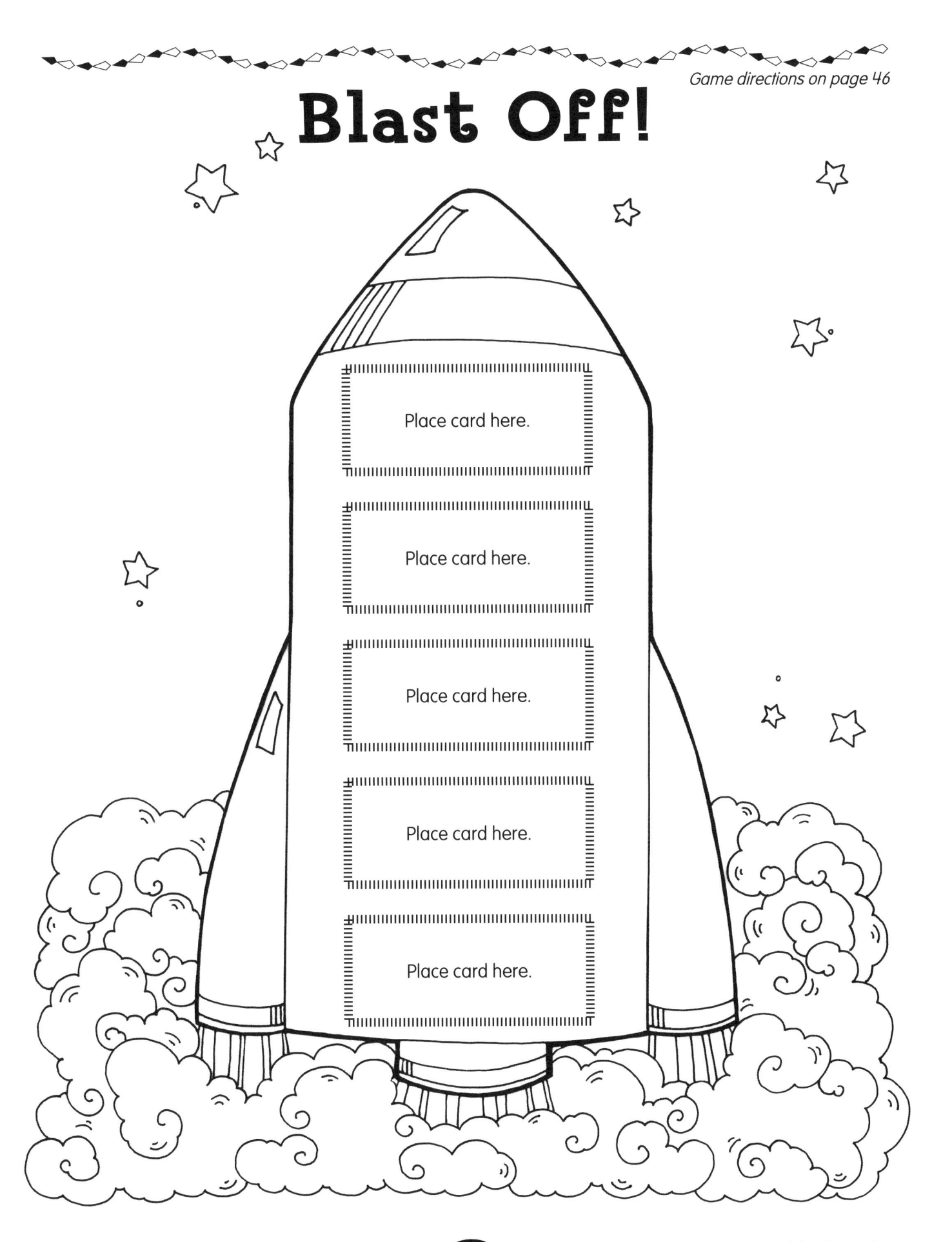

Game directions on page 46

Place card here.

Place card here.

Place card here.

Place card here.

Place card here.

Blast Off!
Game directions on page 46

1 0 0	1 0 1	7 0 0	7 0 7
2 0 0	2 0 2	8 0 0	8 0 8
3 0 0	3 0 3	9 0 0	9 0 9
4 0 0	4 0 4	☆ 653	0 0 0
5 0 0	5 0 5	☆ 389	0 0 0
6 0 0	6 0 6	☆ 163	0 0 0

☆ 206	☆ 312	☆ 409	☆ 514
☆ 627	☆ 780	☆ 530	☆ 960
☆ 135	☆ 891	☆ 245	☆ 322
☆ 428	☆ 575	☆ 664	☆ 702
☆ 844	☆ 983	☆ 117	☆ 298
☆ 474	☆ 671	☆ 768	☆ 856

Specific Skills: Place Value

Ten Dollars and Ten Cents

Game directions on page 46

thousands	hundreds	tens	ones
1,000¢	100¢	10¢	1¢
10 dollar bill	1 dollar bill	dime	penny

Ten Dollars and Ten Cents
Game directions on page 46

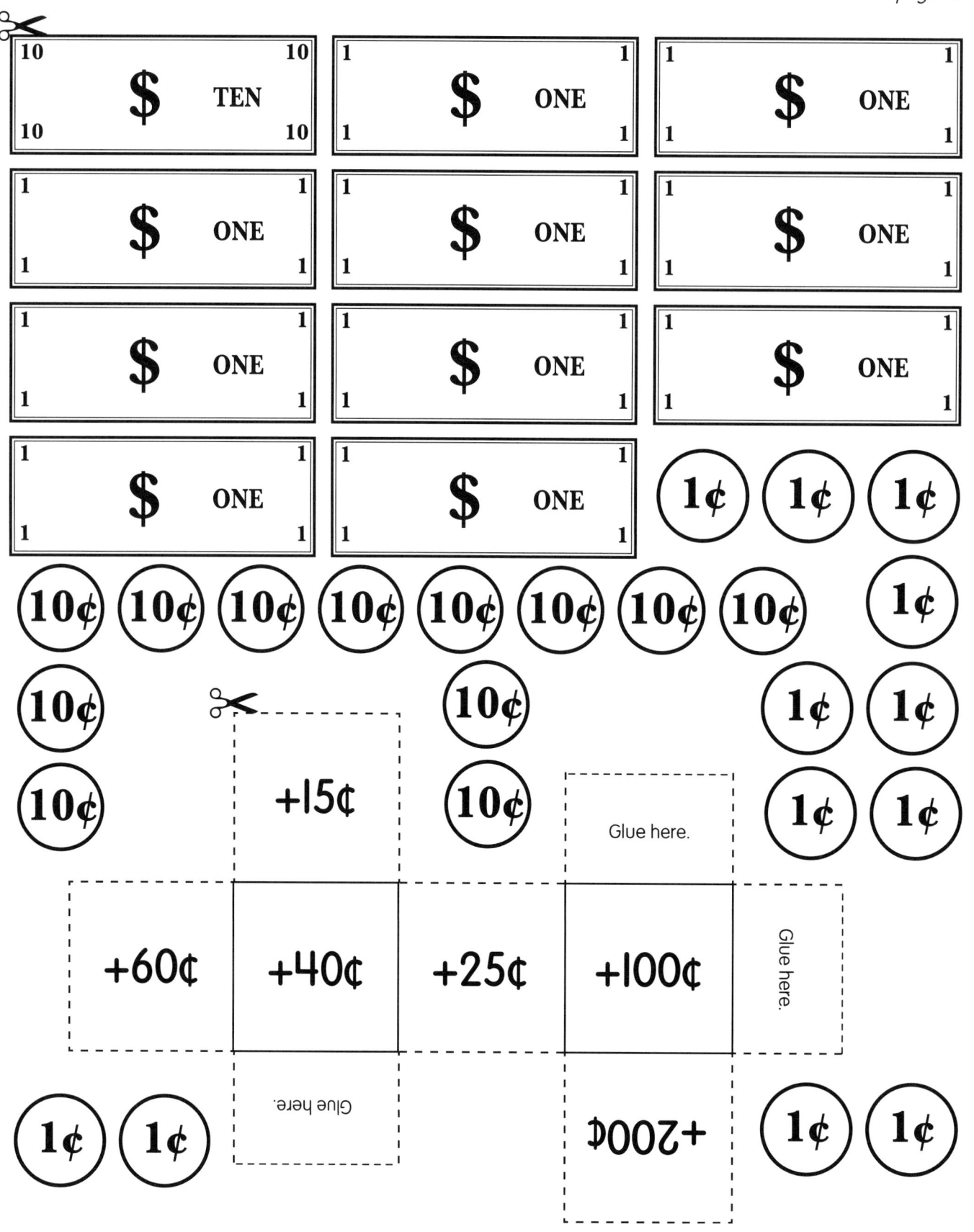

+15¢

+60¢ +40¢ +25¢ +100¢

+200¢

Specific Skills: Place Value

Name _____   Date _____

Money, Money! A Center Activity

To the teacher: Provide a copy of the game board (page 55) and money pieces (page 56) with this page.

Key

penny = 1¢ = $0.01   dime = 10¢ = $0.10   dollar bill = 100¢ = $1.00
(ones)   ten pennies   one hundred pennies

ten dollar bill = 1,000¢ = $10.00
one thousand pennies

Direction: Use dollars, dimes, and pennies to solve the following problems.

1. 400 pennies equal _____ dollars.   _____

2. Solve: 1 dollar + 7 dimes = _____ pennies.   _____

3. If sixty-seven cents equals 60 + 7, then what is the expanded form of eighty-three cents?   _____

4. Subtract: 5 dollars and 35 cents minus 2 dollars and 10 cents.   _____

5. If 10 dimes have the same value as 1 dollar, how many dimes would equal 4 dollars?   _____

6. If 10 dimes equal 1 dollar in value, how many dimes would 6 dollars equal?   _____

7. Solve with dollars, dimes, and pennies: $3.81 + 2.18 = ? $ ___ . ____

8. What is the standard form? 700 pennies + 10 pennies $ ___ . ____

Write It! Solve It!

Direction: Write three problems about money for a friend to solve on the back of this paper.

Numbers Rule! A Center Activity

To the teacher: Reproduce pages 58 and 59 onto colored card stock. Cut out the cards and label them for a math center activity. If interested, code the back of the cards to make them self-corrrecting and then laminate them to make them durable.

Label for the storage envelope

Numbers Rule!

Directions: Study each "A" card. Determine the rule that applies to each set of numbers. Find the rule on a "B" card to match each "A" card!

A
792 
782
772

A
nine hundred nine
↓
909

A
894
−394

A 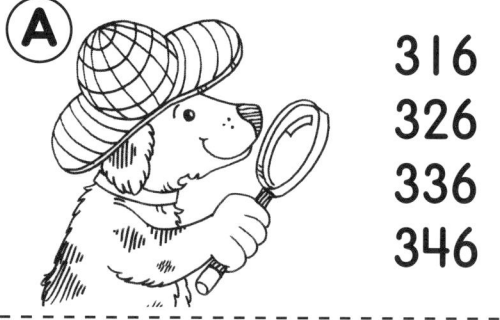
316
326
336
346

A 
526
↓
500 + 20 + 6

A 
282
↓
782

KE-804036 © Key Education — 58 — Specific Skills: Place Value

Numbers Rule! A Center Activity

A	58, 62, 66, 70, 74	A	975, 843, 792
 B	Skip count by 4	 B	Standard form to expanded form
 B	Skip count by 10s	 B	Subtracting to find the difference
 B	Ordered — greatest to least	 B	Count backwards by 10s
 B	Written form to standard form	 B	500 more

Specific Skills: Place Value

Place Value Flash Cards

To the teacher: Copy the flash cards onto colored card stock. Cut them out for use in a math center.

Name the value of the underlined digit.	Name the value of the underlined digit.
31<u>5</u>	<u>4</u>70

Name the value of the underlined digit.	Name the value of the underlined digit.
9<u>6</u>2	<u>8</u>16

Name the value of the underlined digit.	Name the value of the underlined digit.
3<u>0</u>7	52<u>9</u>

KE-804036 © Key Education — 60 — Specific Skills: Place Value

Place Value Flash Cards

To the teacher: Copy the flash cards onto colored card stock. Cut them out for use in a math center.

Which place is the **8** in?

328

Which place is the **4** in?

941

Which place is the **2** in?

203

Which place is the **7** in?

725

Which place is the **5** in?

905

Which place is the **3** in?

836

Specific Skills: Place Value

Web Sites

http://www.dositey.com/addsub/tenoneex.htm

For those children needing to review identifying ones and tens, they can count the pictures and write the correct number in the box.

http://www.gamequarium.com/placevalue.html

This Web site offers a listing of different place value games. For students, the following games and exercises may be appropriate: "Collect Ten" (ten-frame grids) and "Base Ten Blocks" for building numbers up to 999. The "Place Value Puzzler" (easy level) will challenge those students interested in learning about numbers higher than 1000!

http://www.learningbox.com/Base10/CatchTen.html

To play "Catch Ten," the player must click on the base-ten unit cubes as they float down the river. BT Bear stands ready to catch those blocks. When he has enough to make a strip of ten, he will toss the blocks on shore and then wait to catch some more. A great review for children before introducing them to the hundred flat!

http://www.edhelper.com/place_value.htm

Internet (printable) worksheets for teachers and parents can be found at this site.

http://www.arcytech.org/java/b10blocks/

This site offers a great interactive place value screen for kids. Be sure to click on the "name" button first to learn about each feature.

http://www.eduplace.com/math/mathsteps/2/a/

This site has a good explanation of place value for teachers and parents to use as a reference. This site also offers "tips and tricks" and suggestions for how to answer your students' questions.

http://mathforum.org/library/drmath/sets/elem_place_value.html

Dr. Math is the best! You can use this site for all kinds of math questions, and of course, Dr. Math answers place value questions.

Answer Key

Page 5
1. B, 2. A, 3. C, 4. C, 5. A, 6. B

Page 6
7. A, 8. C, 9. C, 10. C, 11. A, 12. B

Page 13
A. 37, B. 62, C. 54, D. 48
Bottom of page: A. 37, 38, 39, 40; B. 62, 63, 64, 65;
C. 54, 55, 56, 57; D. 48, 49, 50, 51

Page 14
A. 4 tens, 5 ones, 45; B. 7 tens, 0 ones, 70; C. 2 tens, 2 ones, 22; D. 3 tens, 9 ones, 39; E. 6 tens, 4 ones, 64; F. 5 tens, 8 ones, 58; G. 9 tens, 5 ones, 95; H. 7 tens, 3 ones, 73
Bottom of page:
Row 1: 33, 43, 53; Row 2: 54, 64, 74;
Row 3: 79, 89, 99

Page 15
1. F; 2. G; 3. A; 4. D; 5. C; 6. H; 7. E; 8. B;
9. 36, 46, 56, 66, 76, 86; 10. 78, 88, 98, 108, 118, 128;
11. 59, 69, 79, 89, 99, 109; 12. 64, 74, 84, 94, 104, 114

Page 16
A. 49, 40 + 9; B. 87, 80 + 7; C. 72, 70 + 2;
D. 56, 50 + 6; E. 60 + 5; F. 90 + 3; G. 20 + 8; H. 30 + 1

Page 17
A. 4 tens drawn, 3 dots drawn, odd;
B. 3 tens drawn, 6 dots drawn, even;
C. 5 tens drawn, 1 dot drawn, odd; D. even, E. odd;
F. even; G. odd; H. even; I. odd; J. even; K. odd;
L. odd; M. even; N. even; O. odd; P. even

Page 18
A. <, B. >, C. <, D. >, E. =, F. <,
G. >; Drawings will vary. H. <; Drawings will vary.

Page 19
1. 300, 2. 600, 3. 200, 4. 500, 5. 400
Bottom of page: 100, 200, 300, 400, 500, 600, 700, 800, 900

Page 20
Check student's drawing.

Page 21
Row 1: 20, 40, 60, 80, 100; Row 2: 120, 140, 160, 180, 200; Row 3: 220, 240, 260, 280, 300; Row 4: 320, 340, 360, 380, 400; Row 5: 420, 440, 460, 480, 500; Row 6: 520, 540, 560, 580, 600; Row 7: 620, 640, 660, 680, 700; Row 8: 720, 740, 760, 780, 800; Row 9: 820, 840, 860, 880, 900; Row 10: 920, 940, 960, 980, 1000
Bottom of page: A. 36, 26, 16, 6; B. 62, 52, 42, 32;
C. 157, 147, 137, 127

Page 22
Hiker on the left: 105; Middle hiker: 103; Hiker on the right: 101
The hiker on the left side is circled.

Page 23
B. 3 hundreds, 6 tens, 0 ones, 360; B. 5 hundreds, 4 tens, 0 ones, 540; D. 2 hundreds, 0 tens, 0 ones, 200; E. 1 hundred, 2 tens, 0 ones, 120; F. 6 hundreds, 4 tens, 0 ones, 640; G. 4 hundreds, 1 ten, 0 ones, 410; H. 3 hundreds, 3 tens, 0 ones, 330

Page 24
A. 1 hundred, 7 tens, 3 ones, 173; B. 2 hundreds, 5 tens, 4 ones, 254; C. 3 hundreds, 1 ten, 2 ones, 312; D. 1 hundred, 4 tens, 5 ones, 145; E. 5 hundreds, 5 tens, 550; F. 4 hundreds, 9 tens, 6 ones, 496
Bottom of page: 550, 496, 312, 254, 173, 145

Page 25
B. 273, C. 425, D. 524, E. 350, F. 408
Bottom of page: 273, 346, 350, 408, 425, 524

Page 26
Check student's drawings.

Page 27
Cat's total: 420; Dog's total: 475; Snake's total: 440; Duck's total: 457

Answer Key

Page 28
1. 17, 2. 33, 3. 67, 4. 91, 5. 120, 6. 244, 7. 338, 8. 506, 9. 652, 10. 875
Answer to riddle: "Little juicy fly foo..."

Page 29
A. 23; B. 39; C. 67; D. 180; E. 200; F. 355; G. 38, 39; H. 50, 51; I. 175, 176; J. 200, 201; K. 210, 211; L. 460, 461; M. 689, 690; N. 800, 801; O. 910, 911

Page 30
Check student's coloring.

Page 31
1. >, 2. >, 3. =, 4. <, 5. <, 6. >, 7. =, 8. =, 9. >, 10. >, 11. <, 12. <

Page 32
B. 190, 188, 179; C. 252, 225, 107; D. 500, 445, 333; E. 642, 628, 602; F. 924, 914, 904; G. 166, 178, 182; H. 91, 98, 104; I. 221, 239, 266; J. 403, 555, 607; K. 699, 720, 757; L. 808, 819, 831

Page 33
A. 400 + 7; B. 200 + 20 + 9; C. 600 + 50 + 8; D. 900 + 20 + 6; E. 300 + 70 + 1; F. 500 + 40
Bottom of page: Answers will vary.

Page 34
A. 246, 200 + 40 + 6; B. 709, 700 + 0 + 9; C. 930, 900 + 30 + 0; D. 457, 400 + 50 + 7; E. 100 + 80 + 5; F. 500 + 60 + 0; G. 400 + 0 + 2; H. 600 + 20 + 7

Page 35
A. 4, 24; B. 85, 105; C. 95, 115; D. 245, 265; E. 893, 913; F. 0, 100; G. 50, 150; H. 200, 300; I. 350, 450; J. 600, 700; K. 0, 200; L. 207, 407; M. 462, 662; N. 629, 829; O. 713, 913; P. 503, 703; Q. 784, 984

Page 36
A. hundreds place, B. tens place, C. ones place, D. tens place, E. hundreds place, F. ones place, G. ones place, H. tens place, J. one hundred sixty-seven, K. three hundred fifty-one, L. six hundred nine, M. eight hundred forty, N. four hundred seventy-five

Page 37
1. 381, 2. 36 and 90, 3. 77, 4. 800, 5. 128, 6. 565, 7. 52, 8. 914, 9. 203

Page 39
A. 98, B. 179, C. 393, D. 378, E. 397, F. 438, G. 652

Page 40
1. 48, 2. 997, 3. 489, 4. 649, 5. 597, 6. 866, 7. 798, 8. 979, 9. 687

Page 41
1. 525, 2. 413, 3. 585, 4. 752, 5. 850, 6. 917

Page 42
A. 243, B. 324, C. 10, D. 329, E. 512, F. 174, G. 210, H. 200

Page 43
1. 31, 2. 33, 3. 66, 4. 52, 5. 230, 6. 431, 7. 540, 8. 403

Page 44
1. 305, 2. 338, 3. 261, 4. 228, 5. 489, 6. 173

Page 57
1. 4, 2. 170, 3. 80 + 3, 4. 3 dollars and 25 cents, 5. 40, 6. 60, 7. $5.99, 8. $7.10